HINKLEY COUNTY

Craig Sullivan

Llumina
Press

Author notes:

This story is fiction. All names (with exception of nationally known brands), locations (with exception of national landmarks), and general descriptions were inspired by the imagination of the author. Unfortunately, the characters portrayed, although completely fictional, can be found in most rural county government offices.

ISBN: 978-1-60594-082-3 (PB)
978-1-60594-083-0 (HC)
978-1-60594-084-7 (Ebook)

Printed in the United States of America by Llumina Press

Library of Congress Control Number: 2008904511

WELCOME
HINKLEY
COUNTY

Chapter 1

The Hinkley County Courthouse meeting room smelled like a three-day-old baloney sandwich. The only window was sealed shut with caulk that appeared to have been applied with a boat oar. Commissioner Sadinski rubbed his hand against his nose under the pretense of playing with his mustache, trying to determine if the foul smell was the result of anything he had handled while cleaning out his dog pen before the meeting. He glanced under the table at his boots and saw nothing clinging to them other than the usual mud and sand.

Chet Sadinski, lean and well proportioned for his age, with thinning silver hair and a seductive smile that enticed voters and scared away potential political opponents, presided over the Hinkley County commissioners' monthly meeting with his fellow county commissioners Ralph Bellows and Syd Featherstone, each seated at the portable front table. The room was small and accommodated only a few ill-arranged folding chairs giving the appearance that the prior meeting might have ended in a fire drill.

Two members of the local media, one from the twice-weekly newspaper the *Hinkley Messenger* and the other from WERM, a local classic country radio station, sat near the back wall trading whispers and leaking occasional perverse outbursts of laughter as they waited for the meeting to begin. Mabel Hinkley, the recording secretary for the commissioners, a matronly woman well into her seventies with her hair in a net and the demeanor of a cornered raccoon, sat at a desk in the corner neatly arranging her paperwork next to a small tape recorder. Mabel had been the secretary for the commissioners' office for over fifty years, primarily because she bore the right last name. She claimed she was directly descended from the Hinkleys that first settled in the area, although the county museum curator disputed her contention—but only in private company.

Featherstone leaned toward Sadinski. "Chet, is that Mabel that smells? I thought we motioned to have the window air conditioner in this room fixed at the last meeting. At least we could have a fan that pushed the air in another direction."

Mabel glanced at the three men huddled together and Featherstone leaned back and smiled, tilting his head in recognition, as if they were discussing her next pay raise. Mabel smiled back, revealing that she had decided to forgo wearing her upper bridge for the meeting. Her three remaining upper front teeth gave her a facial expression similar to an aging groundhog.

Sadinski looked around the room and decided there was not going to be much public interest in today's meeting, so he motioned to Mabel by twirling his index finger to turn on the recorder.

Mabel pushed the button and struggled to gain her balance as she stood, grunting under the strain, and started the meeting with her usual formal opening. "All rise. This commences the August meeting of the Hinkley County commissioners for the good people of Hinkley County. We will begin by reciting the Pledge of Allegiance." Mabel put her hand to her heart and turned to face the flag that usually stood in the corner behind her desk. The flag was gone. "Shit fire. Someone stole the flag."

The two reporters chuckled as Mabel became increasingly agitated and pushed the off button on the recorder.

Sadinski said, "Hell, Mabel, we can pledge without the flag. Just pretend there's a flag there. Turn on the damn recorder, and let's get this goin'. It'll soon be lunch time."

The seconds necessary for Mabel to restart the recorder were punctuated by a snort and loud gasp coming from Commissioner Ralph Bellows' mouth. He had fallen asleep, which was normal for Bellows because by ten o'clock, the official start of the monthly meeting, he had already consumed several belts of bourbon and a couple of beer chasers to calm his nerves in preparation for his public appearance. Sadinski leaned over and gave a stiff elbow to Bellows' shoulder, enough of a jolt to bring him around, at least long enough for him to stand for the pledge.

The pledge was completed, and everyone settled back for what was expected to be a very short meeting. Sadinski shuffled some papers that Mabel had placed in front of him without actually reading any of the fine print and finally looked up and said, "Mabel, is there anything here that needs our attention?"

"Well—" Mabel adjusted her reading glasses and squinted to read her notes. "The county sanitary engineer says the toilet in the, uh, grandstand at the fairgrounds, uh, is all fouled up. Or maybe it's plugged up or something. He needs to call Moses Callahan to bring his dippin' machine and clean it out, but Moses won't come unless he gets paid cash on the spot. Say's 'You guys'—this'n is his words, not mine—'You guys don't pay worth a damn.'"

The local newspaper reporter was laughing so hard he could not take the notes necessary to get the quote straight. The young female reporter from the radio station fumbled with her tape recorder to make sure the tape was still running and operational, not wanting to miss the opportunity to use Mabel's quote on her noon newscast.

Sadinski glanced at Featherstone with a look of disgust and then back at Mabel. There was no use looking at Bellows since he had fallen into a deep slumber, his head tilted back against the wall. "Damn it, Mabel, tell Wally to get somebody else, or get some of those guys sittin' around the garage to go out there and clean it up. Syd, you want to make a motion about that?"

"Well, dad gum it, I think I do." Featherstone scratched his chin. "I move that we get somebody else, or fix the dad gum thing ourselves."

"All in favor say aye. There you go, Mabel. Anything else?" Sadinski said impatiently, not waiting for a consenting vote from the one commissioner that was still conscious.

"Well, uh, there's a letter here from somebody named Sh—Sh—Shit, uh, Shit Head."

"What? Let me see that." Sadinski stood up, tried without success to get around Bellows, who continued to snore with his legs stretched under the table, turned and walked around Featherstone and over to Mabel. He snatched the letter from her hand with apparent disgust and held it out to arm's length to get a bead on the fine print. "Let's see. John Sh—Sh—Shi-thead. It's Shi-thead. The last part of the name is pronounced like laid or trade; it's Shi-thead. Jesus H. Christ, Mabel, don't put that in the minutes. Let's see, what's Mr. Shi-thead want?" he said drawing emphasis to the pronunciation. Sadinski read the letter and then read it again as he took his seat.

"This here gentleman is from the Department of Homeland Security and Emergency Management. That would be the federal government. He's a-wanting us to set up a regional county department of homeland security. Says the feds are requiring it and will pay for it. Let's see, somewhere here he said he would be coming to visit the head of our homeland security department. Here it is—the first Tuesday after the second Monday of August."

Featherstone scratched his chin again and said in a low growl, "What the hell kind of talk is that?"

"That, my friend, is federal government talk," Sadinski responded. "Let's see, this here's the first Wednesday after the first Monday, so that means he will be here—anyway, he's coming to talk to us sometime this month. Mabel, put that on our calendar."

Bellows snorted, gasped for a breath of air, swatted a fly from his cheek, and settled back against the wall.

Featherstone leaned over to Sadinski and whispered, "Chet, it sounds like he don't want to see us, he wants to see our head of homeland security, which I don't think we got, do we?"

Mabel looked up and pointed her finger at the tape recorder, saying, "You have to speak up if you want this thing to work. It ain't gonna record you two whispering to each other."

Sadinski thought for a long minute and said, "Don't get your shorts all bunched up, Mabel. Okay, gentlemen, what we need is an executive session. This is important federal business here, dealing with terrorists and such and ain't something that should be right out in the open for every lowlife to know about. Mabel, shut that thing off and clear the room. We're goin' into executive session." Sadinski turned to Bellows who was making low gasping sounds. "Wake up, Ralph."

Sadinski elbowed Bellows again and he sat up abruptly and said, "Aye. Are we adjourned?" He looked at Sadinski through bloodshot eyes for approval. "Where we goin' for lunch?" It was tradition for the commissioners' expense account to buy lunch after every scheduled meeting.

The two news people filed out into the hall and Mabel shut the door. She slowly walked back to the desk and started to turn on the recorder, and Sadinski cleared his throat the way one does when you really don't have to. Mabel looked up and Sadinski shook his head, indicating he did not want the session recorded.

"Ralph, we're not goin' to lunch yet; we're discussing this letter from the feds. Syd, you sure we don't have anyone that's supposed to be taking care of this? Seems like there should have been someone," Sadinski said, studying the letter again. "Ralph, you know anything about this?"

"About what?" Bellows said, straightening his tie and picking at a spot that looked like egg yolk where the tie rested on his belly.

"About this damn letter we've been discussing, homeland security, terrorists, and such."

Bellows abruptly sat up, his cheeks puffed out like a hooked blowfish. "Terrorists, what terrorists? Goddamn, we need to do something. Get the sheriff in here. Maybe we need the National Guard. Call the governor." His hands were shaking as he rubbed them together, and his bulbous nose turned purple as he looked out of the dirty window at the bar and grill across the street from the courthouse. He licked his dry lips a time or two and said, "Damn, I got to go use the head. You go on discussin'. I'll be right back."

With that, he pushed the table away from his chair and hurried out of the room. Sadinski sat for a moment and watched through the grimy window as Bellows came into view hurrying across the street and went into the After Hours Lounge.

"Damn. By tomorrow, the whole county's going to be talking about terrorists, and we don't even have a director," Sadinski said, turning back to the letter on the table. "We can't let this thing get out of control. By the time Sh—Shi-thead gets here, we need to have a director and act like we know what's going on."

"Why don't we let the sheriff take care of this?" Featherstone asked. "He's the big shot in the county. He'd love to make a big deal out of this, talking to the feds and all. Hell, by the time Sh-whatever shows up, he could have several terrorists locked up for inspection."

Sadinski pictured the sheriff parading Shi-thead around the county, showing him all the potential terrorist targets, eating expensive lunches, arranging trips to Washington to learn how to uncover terrorist plots, meeting with congressmen, and maybe even the president. "No, I don't think that's a good idea. I mean, Sheriff Minor is real busy with the immigration thing, trying to keep the Mexicans from opening too many restaurants, and besides, I think we should take control of this new department, personally handle it, play it real close to the belt." Sadinski leaned over to Featherstone, lowering his voice, making Mabel immediately reach to adjust her hearing aid. "Besides, this could turn out to be real good for you and me, if we play it right. I smell federal money, if you know what I mean."

Featherstone smiled, knowing from experience that Sadinski must have a plan, and he was included. "Who do you think we ought to appoint director?" Featherstone asked in a raised voice, giving Mabel acknowledgement that she was now being included in the conversation.

Just then, the door jarred open and Boog Simpson, the courthouse custodian, backed into the room, pulling a mop bucket by the mop handle behind him. Boog stopped halfway in, his rear end inside, and his head still sticking out of the door into the hallway, apparently thinking the room was unoccupied and he was mostly hidden from those waiting in the hall. He scratched himself, reaching into his county-rented coveralls, and after the last full scratch broke wind in a well tuned flatulence that seemed to resound off the walls of the small meeting room. Boog chuckled a little, his head still protruding from the door and started to move his entire body back into the hall.

"Boog," Sadinski yelled. "Get back in here."

Boog almost jumped out of his coveralls. He wheeled around and stuck his head through the crack in the door. His eyes shown wide and his mouth stood open as he glanced around the room. Mabel fiddled with the papers on her desk, apparently trying to act as if she hadn't noticed the intrusion while Sadinski and Featherstone eyed him with serious lack of understanding.

Jasper Simpson, commonly known as Boog, was a fixture in the courthouse. Most thought he actually lived there since he wasn't known to have any family still living in the county. At some time prior to the current commissioners' administration, he had been given the position of custodian by a sympathetic county administrator, who felt it was good stewardship as trustee of the county's money to put Boog to work inside the courthouse instead of paying someone to watch him inside the county jail, which was where everyone felt he would eventually end up. Boog showed up for work every day, and as long as the county supplied him with fresh coveralls once a week, he maintained a reasonable appearance and kept the courthouse hallways clear of debris. He was friendly to most and overly courteous to the women that worked in the county offices. Boog didn't drink or smoke, and it was common to see him in the city square feeding pigeons or at the city park watching a little league baseball game. He was around forty by anyone's estimate and was thought to have the mental capacity of a ten-year-old. He had been called Booger since his first day in school and had matured to Boog when his size dictated some respect. He had unruly, brown, curly hair, a fair complexion, a pleasant, boyish smile, was of a height that brought a good broom handle to his shoulder, and he spent a good portion of his working life leaning on one in some obscure corner of the courthouse.

"Boog, come on back in here, boy." Sadinski changed his tone to one of accommodation. "You might as well suffer along with the rest of us in this little room."

"Jesus, Boog," Featherstone added. "Couldn't you do that down the hall?"

"Jeez, I'm real sorry, Mr. Featherstone. I didn't know you all were in here. The door was shut, and all the other people left. I thought the meeting was over." Boog waved his hand in the air, trying frantically to dissipate the smell. Everyone stayed silent for a long moment, and finally, Boog retreated to the corner of the room and took a seat. "I guess I'll just sit here for a spell, if that's all right."

"It's all right, Boog," Sadinski said. "Just try to hold any more of that until we get through."

There was another long silence until Featherstone said, "You were saying we ought to keep this close to the hip. That mean you are going be the director?"

"No, we can't appoint ourselves department head, especially when we are the ones making the new department. No, we need a figurehead, someone to head up the department but not do anything. Hell, there won't be any employees, there won't be any budget, there won't be anything to do except answer the phone if anyone from Washington calls, and Stella on the switchboard can handle that—just say there's nobody in right now. We don't want to hire anyone from the outside; that would be a waste of the federal government's money," Sadinski said in a sarcastic tone. "And if there's some big doings, like in Washington or something, we can always appoint one of us the official county representative."

Featherstone started to see where Sadinski was leading him. "So, we kind of run things from behind the scene, making sure everything is the way the feds want it, and if there's a few crumbs that fall off the cart, we—I mean, the county—can take advantage of it."

"That's kind of the way I was thinking this might go. We just have to come up with a department head before Shi-thead comes to give us the scoop on how this whole scam—I mean program—works." Sadinski leaned back in his chair, folding his hands on his stomach, and looked at the ceiling. "We need someone to accept this position but not let it go to his head. Understand that it's just a name. Kind of like the superintendent of sewers, you are a superintendent, but you still have to clean the sewers."

Sadinski and Featherstone looked across the room at Boog and then looked at each other and smiled. A high five was in order, but they both knew it would not be appropriate.

Chapter 2

The final air bubble was removed from the stick-on lettering, and the freshly cleaned fogged glass insert in the office door gleamed with the title Office of Homeland Security, Hinkley County. The office was a converted storage room next to the commissioners' office where they formerly had stored discarded office equipment and new supplies. Sadinski and Featherstone debated whether to put Boog's name on the door and decided it might be a little extreme. Besides, if this appointment didn't work out in the first few days, they could change the plan and find another stooge. They did have a local engraver make a nameplate to sit on the small desk identifying Jasper Simpson.

After much discussion and negotiation as to who would be the primary recipient of future benefits, if any, and how the anticipated windfall was to be distributed, the three commissioners called Boog into their private office.

Boog leaned on a broom near the door of the office, assuming an emergency cleanup was needed, which was common, given Bellows' usual inebriated condition and his propensity to stumble into things. Sadinski smiled and pointed toward the lone chair in front of his desk. Each commissioner had a desk, all arranged in a semi-circle, with Sadinski's in the middle. "Boog, take a seat. We want to talk to you a bit."

Boog held his ground, sensing a good verbal thrashing was in the works, making eye contact with each man before saying, "I'm really sorry about that thing in the meeting room the other day. I know I did wrong. I won't do it again. I mean, I'll go down the hall to the men's room. You ain't gonna fire me, are you?" His voice took on a pleading tone. "For a little fart? That don't seem fair. I've heard Miss Hinkley fart right in her chair outside your office, and she didn't get fired."

"Slow down, Boog. Nobody is going to get fired," Sadinski responded. "Come over here and sit down a spell. Actually, we want to tell you how much we appreciate the great job you do. You've been with the county, what, fifteen years?"

Boog looked at each commissioner, shifting his weight from one foot to the other, and finally leaned the broom against the wall, walked to the chair, and sat down. "'Bout that."

Sadinski continued, "If the worst thing you have ever done is fart in a commissioners' meeting, that's a pretty good record." Featherstone and Bellows both nodded their heads, affirming the conclusion.

"We think it's time for you to move up in this organization, so to speak. We would like to give you a new position, an important position. Now, mind you, it won't pay any more than you currently make. The county just doesn't have any money available for a raise, not right now, anyway. But that's not to say that if you do well and do what we tell you to do, there might not be a little extra for you at Christmas time. What do you think about that?"

Boog again looked with suspicion at all three men. "What I gotta do?"

"Nothing, really," Sadinski said. "Just work with us, kind of like our personal assistant. You will have your own office right up here on the top floor of the courthouse. Just do what you do now, show up for work every day, and keep the offices clean. You'll have to wear normal clothes sometimes, not the coveralls. I think we can help you with that expense." The other two men again nodded their heads in affirmation. "Boog, you've heard about all this terrorist stuff, right?"

Boog kept silent, but gave a short, affirmative headshake.

"Well, some guys in Washington think we need to keep an eye out for, you know, terrorists. Even though we all know we don't have any around here, they are saying we need to have someone act as if they're looking. We figured that would be a good job for you, along with keeping the offices clean."

Boog continued to make eye contact with all three men. "You're kidding, right? This here is some kind of spoof, like the auditor did when he said there was a rat in the ladies toilet? It ended up being a furry stuffed toy like you win at the fair that he put in there. Like that, huh? Sure, I'll go along with it, if that's what you want me to do, so long as I still got a job. I do, don't I? I ain't fired?"

"Good boy, Boog," Sadinski said. "Congratulations, you're the new director of Homeland Security and Emergency Management for Hinkley County. Come on, boys, let's show Boog his new office."

Everyone stood and ushered Boog to the door, went through Mabel's office into the hall, and stood in front of the door stenciled "Homeland Security."

"This is your new office, Boog." Sadinski opened the door and reached for the string on the light dangling on a wire from the ceiling. Boog stepped forward, leaned into the door, and his eyes immediately focused on the nameplate in the middle of the small desk, Jasper Simpson. There was only room for one person to enter and get around the desk to the wooden straight-back chair. Then Boog had to straddle the chair like getting on a horse because there was not enough room to pull the chair back from the desk.

All Boog could say was, "Som-bitch, this is my office? Som-bitch; I ain't never had my own office. Sorry, I didn't mean—I mean, I didn't mean to cuss but this is, well, it's my office, huh? This is where I go from now on? Director of Homeland Security, that's me?"

Bellows spoke up for the first time. "Boog, now let's not get all high and mighty here. It's just a title. As we said, someone had to do it, so that person is you. Nothing has changed; you're still Boog. Look, fellas, I have to go. Uh, I have another meeting. Boog, you take care now, and don't go tellin' many people about this. We don't want the terrorists to know we're watching them." He turned and walked down the hall, chuckling.

"Don't mind him, Boog," Featherstone said. "He just wants to keep this a little quiet until we get everything ready for the big announcement. Now, this Wednesday, the representative from the federal government's Office of Homeland Security is coming to visit us and meet with you. You won't have to do much, just shake his hand and smile."

"We'll be right there with you, Boog," Sadinski added. "So you will have to dress up a bit, okay? Get a clean shirt and some pants that aren't, you know, all stained." Sadinski pulled a twenty-dollar bill out of his wallet and gave it to Boog. "Go over to the Super Value and get a shirt. One with a collar," he said sternly. "And Boog, remember, you don't talk unless I ask you to. You just smile and stay back. Oh, yeah, and keep the damned courthouse clean, too. You are still the janitor."

The euphoria Boog felt over the last few minutes was fading fast as Sadinski seemed to slide from the sympathetic bearer of good tidings to the overbearing jerk Boog had always known him to be. Still, this was his new office, and he had something he had never had in his life—a title. Director of Homeland Security and Emergency Management, Hinkley County.

"Yes, sir, I'll keep this place cleaner 'n ever, especially my office—and y'all's, too."

Sadinski sighed and turned to Featherstone as they walked back to their office. "I don't know if this feels right. He's stupid as a river rock, but a slippery river rock can trip you up faster than a ground lizard." He fetched his hat off the coat rack and placed it neatly on his head, giving the wide brim a slight pull, Texan style. "I guess we'll find out Wednesday."

Chapter 3

Boog was sitting in his office, pushing his nameplate from one end of the small desk to the other, talking to himself in a whisper. "If it's here, you can see it from the elevator. If it's here, you can see it from Miss Hinkley's door. If it's in the middle, somebody walking by will see me and the name at the same time." He had been sitting at the desk since 6:30 AM, after he arrived and unlocked the service entrance of the courthouse. It was now 9:00, and most of the offices were occupied on the lower floors. The upper floor was occupied by the commissioners' suite and other small offices that were seldom used, like the office belonging to the Tri-County Regional Recycling coordinator, who was actually the landfill operator and had an office in an abandoned travel trailer at the dump. Next to that unused office was the Hinkley County Regional Airport operations manager, who actually lived next to the grass airstrip and kept it mowed for twenty dollars a month.

The offices did have greater significance than just the prestige of a name on a door. The position of Tri-County Regional Recycling Coordinator was funded by the state through a federal grant to promote recycling. The county received two hundred thousand dollars each year to be distributed to each of the three counties participating. The Hinkley County commissioners received an extra twenty thousand dollars to maintain the office and pay the coordinator. Over the years, the annual extra compensation to pay the coordinator had faded from the county auditor's memory and from the county receipt book as well, since some time ago it had inadvertently been made payable directly to the Office of the Hinkley County Commissioners and placed in their discretionary expense account.

The Hinkley County Regional Airport operations manager position was funded by the Federal Aviation Administration and had started out as a grant applied for and awarded to an energetic, newly-elected, one-term commissioner to investigate the feasibility of building an airport to attract a regional air carrier. Of course, the grant included enough money for a professional consultant charging an enormous fee to drive to Hinkley County from the state capital and spend a week in the Hinkley Motor Lodge conducting a feasibility study. He eventually wrote a report stating that unless Hinkley County's population quadrupled within the next five years or General Motors Corporation decided to move their corporate headquarters to Hinkley County, there was no need for an enlarged or paved airstrip in Hinkley County.

When the grant money was exhausted, no one except the long-serving, re-elected commissioners seemed to notice that the position of Hinkley County Regional Airport operations manager continued to be funded by the FAA. Not only was it funded, it received the generous federally mandated ten percent inflationary increase each year and now could almost pay for a paved runway with each annual allocation, if the commissioners thought it was needed, which they did not. So the check was conveniently deposited into the commissioners' discretionary fund each year to pay for unfunded expenses that from time to time arose. Like the need for a four-wheel-drive, front-end loading, sixty-inch cutting surface lawn tractor to replace the one purchased last year, which had completely broken down beyond repair and ended up in Sadinski's barn.

Featherstone exited the elevator and walked past the new office of the Homeland Security director just as Boog was trying to snatch an errant nose hair that had been tickling his upper lip all morning. Both looked surprised as their eyes met and Featherstone just shook his head and continued into his office. "Hey, Mabel."

"Good morning, Mister Featherstone," Mabel responded.

"Dad gum weather doesn't know what it wants to do," Featherstone said, looking through his in-box. "Nothing much here, I see. Heard anything from the fed? What time he will be here?"

"No, but Mister Sadinski said you all would be having lunch at the Denny's and that I should call the manager and arrange for the big round table. Sounds like something special is going on."

Featherstone gave a thoughtful look out into the hall. "What's Boog been doing all morning?"

"Haven't seen him come or go all morning. Said hello when I came in and that's it."

"He have clean pants on?" Featherstone asked, straightening his tie.

"I don't know, Mister Featherstone," Mabel responded curtly, as if Boog's dress or hygiene were outside her scope of responsibilities. "And Mister Bellows called and said he would not be in today. He sounded a little under the weather. I think the American Legion stag was last night."

The elevator door chimed, and Sadinski stepped into the hallway, hat tilted forward, his best Sunday suit hanging straight and creased on his well-proportioned body, and shiny leather boots glistening under the fluorescent hall lights. Five steps clicking on the terrazzo floor placed Sadinski in front of Boog, his hands still wrapped around the nameplate, whispering to himself.

"Boog, come out here. Let me see what my twenty bucks did for your appearance." Sadinski stood with his arms crossed looking down at Boog. Boog slowly rose and stepped over his chair and around the desk. He had on a polo shirt that was a little tight around the armpits and maybe one size too small. His pants bunched at his boots, but were for the most part clean and wrinkle free.

"Well, I guess it will have to do. After you spent the five dollars for that shirt, what'd you do with the rest of my money?"

Boog stayed silent, not knowing how to respond since he hadn't even bought the shirt, but used one the church had given him two Christmases ago.

Sadinski gave up the eye contact and chose another subject. "The guy from the feds will be here about eleven. I don't want you in this room. I want the light out, and I want you off cleaning or doing whatever you do during the day. Promptly at eleven-thirty, I want you to come to our office door and check with Mabel. At that point, if I feel it's necessary, I will introduce you to Mister Shi-thead," Sadinski emphasized the pause between the two syllables in Shi-thead's name. "Mabel will tell you what to do—whether to skedaddle or sit and wait for us to call you into the room. Now git." With that, Sadinski turned, went into the commissioners' suite, and closed the hall door. Boog stood in the corridor, apprehensive about his next move. Following instructions was one thing he was good at, so he turned off his office light, closed the door, and headed for the stairs. Might as well check out some of the women using the ladies' restroom for a while.

Chapter 4

John Shi-thead made a grand entrance, pulling up in front of the courthouse in a canary yellow Hummer, pulling a thirty-foot travel trailer. The Hummer was the military version, overly wide and high off the ground with tinted windows providing an ominous presence. It came equipped with brush bar and wench on the front, spare water, fuel, and emergency supply containers secured to the rear door, and topped with an emergency strobe light bar. "Homeland Security" was stenciled on both front doors, and in large letters on the top, for aerial identification, were the initials DHS. The travel trailer was white with giant, yellow-stenciled "Homeland Security" on both sides and DHS on the top. He pulled in curbside, taking up the disabled veteran special parking space and three handicapped loading zone spots. He marched up the steps and into the courthouse with an assistant in tow, carrying a large satchel in one arm and several large binders in the other. Shi-thead had the pace and demeanor of a military man, but his size detracted from the effect. He was around five-foot-three on a good day, even with thick-soled shoes, a hairline that had already receded too far for him to consider late night TV remedies, and trendy wire rimmed glasses. His sleeves were rolled to the elbow, and his silk tie was loose and flapping as he bounced up the stairs.

Boog stood in the corner of the courthouse entrance hall next to the ladies' room and witnessed Shi-thead slam through the front door without regard for his attendant, who had to disassemble her load on the landing at the top of the steps and fumble with the door, holding it with her foot and trying to grapple with the numerous items. Boog rushed to her assistance, picked up most of the binders, and held the door.

"Thank you," the young woman said in a meek voice. She appeared post-college age and very petite. Boog felt he could not only carry her burden but probably her as well. She wore a knee-length business suit with a white brocade blouse, exposing her petite neckline. Her blond hair was cut short and hung straight with a defined part, partially covering her pale face. Boog was immediately struck by her size and appearance, feeling an unfamiliar rush of excitement. Both rushed to catch up with Shi-thead, who had presented himself at the information desk that was equipped with a bell to call for assistance. He slammed his hand on the bell several times, impatiently craning his neck as if expecting a throng of bellhops to appear at his beckoning.

Boog and the young lady stepped up behind Shi-thead, and Boog said, "There ain't anybody around right now. Stella takes her break about now, and besides, hardly anyone needs information around here. If they do, they ask me."

"And who, pray tell, are you?" Shi-thead asked indignantly.

"I'm Bo—Jasper Simpson. I'm the director of homeland security for Hinkley County." Shi-thead looked at the young woman then at Boog, and then back at the young woman.

"You are kidding, right?" Shi-thead said and waited for a reply.

None came.

"Okay, then. I'm John Shi-thead, procurement specialist for the Midwest region of the Department of Homeland Security. This is my executive assistant, Marty Ringwald. We are here to give instruction on utilization of the resources of the federal Department of Homeland Security and Emergency Management. The manuals you are holding will become your bible, so to speak, on how to access the full resources of the federal government. We are talking about the security of our freedom, son, so there is nothing we will not do to counter the sinister forces that wish to undermine the sanctity of what our forefathers gave their lives to protect. We will be right there, standing behind you in case of a terrorist threat, potential plots to pollute our environment, or even an investigation of terrorist cell groups banding together under the guise of a Middle

Eastern restaurant. All you have to do is call Marty—she will be your direct liaison—and let her know what you need. Now, let's go out, and we will show you your official Department of Homeland Security vehicle, courtesy of the Department of Defense." Shi-thead turned and headed back the way he came, leaving Boog and Marty grappling with the binders and satchel.

While walking, Shi-thead kept talking. "The army department of procurement made a little mistake, much to our benefit. They ordered fifteen thousand Hummers to be delivered to Frisco for shipment overseas. Only problem was, none of them had air conditioning. Some schmuck in the procurement department must have really got his ass chewed for that little foul-up. Anyway, they were going to send them all to the shredder until one of our brighter new employees found out about it. Now, here is where you learn a big lesson about the federal government, ah—what was your name again?" They had reached the Hummer and Shi-thead leaned against the high fender with his arms crossed.

"Well my real name is Jasper Simpson, but everyone calls me Boog."

"Boog—like in Booger?" Shi-thead looked at Marty. "Make a note of that. Anyway, Booger, here's your first lesson in how our government works. You would think the smart thing for the army to do would be to give those vehicles to another part of their department, say in Alaska, where they don't need much air conditioning." Shi-thead pointed in a direction he assumed was north. "But they can't do that because that would screw up the budget for procurement of the Alaska guy's stuff. He would have to cancel his order for a thousand Hummers without air, causing the Hummer Company to lay off three thousand workers and putting the whole economy in the crapper. The same thing for us—we can't just ask the army for their screwed up Hummers because they're not part of our federal department or our budget. But here's how mister smart DHS employee—that's short for Department of Homeland Security by the way—got around the problem." He knelt down on one knee as if he was going to scratch out his next play in the dirt.

When no one else knelt, but just stared at him as he looked up, he stood back up and continued. "See, back when Katrina was such a big deal, one of our branch departments, Federal Emergency Management, bought thirteen thousand travel trailers, thinking they would make good temporary housing for the people that got rousted in the flooding. Only problem was, the code in most of the cities where the flood hit would not allow anyone to live in a travel trailer inside the city limits. And outside the city limits, there wasn't any water or power, so the freaking things were useless." Shi-thead had begun flapping his arms in excitement and raising his voice as he built toward the crescendo of his story. "But here's the good part, Booger; our guy files a special emergency request to borrow thirteen thousand Hummers from the army to pull our thirteen thousand travel trailers around the country in case of future disasters. Bingo," he yelled, causing Marty and Boog to take a step back. "We got our Hummers, the army gets to order fifteen thousand more Hummers, the economy keeps on buzzing, and Booger, you get one of your very own, with a trailer attached to boot, and a damn nice trailer, if I may say so myself. It's equipped with everything necessary to sustain a family of four for up to two years without walking outside, as long as you don't mind eating K-rations and freeze-dried spaghetti. And this Hummer is a beauty. It will drive over any terrain this God-forsaken county has to offer and spit it out the exhaust pipe.

"Well, Booger, that's about it. You need to study those manuals, and pay close attention to the red one. That's the procurement manual with all the forms necessary to order equipment. Just send them to Marty; she'll get right on it. And anything else you need or have questions about, just call Marty. Now, you need to take us to your airport so we can get a flight back to Washington."

"Uh, we don't have what you would call an airport," Boog said sheepishly. "The closest real airport is over in Cougar Falls, but they only have a few private planes. Now Johnny Johnston—he lives out on Old 23—he was a war hero and pilot in the air force. He has a plane in his barn that he flies around to check his cattle, but I don't think all three of you would fit in the cockpit."

Shi-thead stood next to the Hummer and studied the sidewalk for a minute. "Okay, take us to the nearest Hertz car rental, and we'll drive to the closest big airport."

Boog leaned against the Hummer, rubbed his chin, and spoke his thoughts. "Far as I know, there ain't any Hertz, or any other car rental places in this county. Now, Fred Ribley, he has the Ford dealership over on the strip; he has loaners, but usually only when he's fixing your car. But we could talk to him. He thought you were thinking about a new Ford, he'd probably loan you one to test drive. I did that once." Boog chuckled and looked at Marty. "It'll only work once though; it don't take him long to figure out when you're only out for a joy ride in one of his new cars."

"Hand me your phone," Shi-thead said, turning to Marty. "It's time to call in reinforcements." Shi-thead stepped away from Boog and Marty and began yelling into the phone, waving his free hand, pointing here and there, and inserting occasional profanity. After several calls, he stopped talking and walked back to the car. "Booger, where's the closest place a helicopter can land? You know, one of those things with a propeller on top instead of in the front," he said, rolling his eyes at Marty.

"Well, let's see. The school yard is just a little ways over there, and school's out for another week until the end of summer."

Shi-thead yelled into the cell phone. "Just put in the coordinates for the county courthouse and look a little west." He turned to Boog with his hand over the phone. "That is west, isn't it?" He returned to the phone. "And you will see a big yellow Hummer with DHS on top. That's right, got it, see you then." He terminated the call and said with authority, "They'll be here in fifteen minutes. Just happens a chopper from the Coast Guard is over near Cougar Falls doing search and rescue for an old couple that drove off a bridge into the river. I told them to drop what they are doing and pick us up. It's not as if the old geezers are lost in the ocean or something. Everyone knows they're there, so a couple of hours aren't going to matter. Get in the truck and get us to the school yard."

Chapter 5

Sadinski and Featherstone stood near the west-facing window of their office and watched a large Coast Guard helicopter approach and land in the schoolyard. Once it slowed to a hover and started dropping for a landing, trees and buildings obscured their sight and they could not see who exited the aircraft. Sadinski turned to Featherstone and said, "Quite an entrance for our guest, wouldn't you say? I love the way the feds do stuff. No screwing around; just get right down to business. Let's get over there before he has a chance to look around and decide to call this deal off and fly back out of here." They rushed out of the office and hurried for the elevator. As they exited the back entrance of the courthouse, they saw the chopper rising into the sky and nosing toward the horizon.

The men double-timed toward their car in the adjoining parking lot, but were jolted to a stop as the yellow Hummer with trailer in tow turned the corner and headed into the parking lot. Boog had the driver's window down and a big smile on his face. Sadinski smoothed his jacket, positioned his hat just right, and walked toward the Hummer, Featherstone following. The tinted windows gave no hint as to the rear seat occupant or occupants.

"Well, Boog, I'm glad to see you were on your toes and picked up our guest, Mister Shi-thead, I presume." Sadinski tried to look through the open window. "Tell them to get out, Boog. We'd like to meet them, and then we're scheduled to have a little ceremony, take a couple pictures, and go to lunch. Hell of a vehicle, huh, Syd?"

"Dad gum right, hell of a vehicle. I didn't know they made 'em with matching trailers. Dad gum hell of a trailer."

Sadinski reached for the back door, opened it with a big smile, and said, "Welcome to Hink— Where the hell is he, Boog?"

The question hit Boog like the time his third-grade teacher asked him in front of the entire class, "Don't you know your ABCs, son?" In all the excitement, he had forgotten to take Shithead to the commissioners' office. He was speechless. "Uh, they just left in that heeliocopter— They were in a big hurry, something about some accident over in Cougar Falls. People drowned, you know." It was close to the truth, something that he felt strongly about.

"What do you mean they left?" Sadinski was beet red, pulling his hat off his head, running his fingers through his scant hair and stamping his foot on the pavement. "Boog, damn it, you were supposed to stay away," he whined. "He probably got one look at you and hightailed out of here."

"Dad gum it, Boog, you don't listen worth a damn." Featherstone turned to look in the direction of the helicopter's path. "There goes our ticket to Washington. I told you it was a bad idea to use Boog for this."

They both turned to walk back toward the courthouse and Sadinski responded, "You thought it was a good idea, just like me. Don't give me that 'It's your fault' business. You've been part of this decision-making process right from the start. My fault, my ass."

Sadinski abruptly stopped, and Featherstone nearly ran over him. Sadinski pushed Featherstone aside and turned to look back at the Hummer and trailer. "Wait a minute," Sadinski said. "They're gone, but that truck and trailer are still here."

Boog had scooted down into the seat so his head was barely visible through the window. As the two men started back, he reached over and hit the up button on the window.

"Boog, put that window back down," Sadinski said sternly. "Now, let's start over. I want to know what happened from the start and how you ended up with this here truck and trailer."

Boog stepped out of the Hummer and began his tale, right down to shaking Marty's little hand before she stepped into the helicopter.

"So you're telling me that this here Hummer and trailer belong to the county now?" Sadinski asked, stepping back so he could get a better view of the equipment. "And there's more where that came from? Damn, did they give you a catalogue or anything?"

"Dad gum it, Boog. It still don't seem right to me that you went off and did this on your own. Chet, it just don't seem right now, dad gum it. I think we ought to put Boog on probation or something. He just can't be goin' off and doing stuff like this, even if it was accidental."

"Okay, calm down, Syd," Sadinski said, putting his arm around Featherstone's shoulder and turning him away from Boog and the truck. "You know, if you analyze this a little, it starts to look better. Maybe what Boog did could end up being the best move. I mean, this guy Shi-thead doesn't even know we exist, so there's no way any accusations could come back to us. I mean, if there is ever an inquiry about anything. I mean, not that we would ever do anything wrong, but say we ordered something from the federal catalogue and somebody asked some questions—hell, it was Boog."

Featherstone glanced at Boog. "Maybe you're right. But it don't hurt to throw a little fear into Boog." He turned to Boog and said, "Okay, we're not going to put you on probation this time, but just keep in mind what I said." Featherstone hitched his pants up in an expression of superiority and again surveyed the equipment. "What are we going to do with this?"

Sadinski rubbed his chin. "I've been considering that. How does this sound? We set the trailer up behind the courthouse with some water and power and move Boog in there. It has to be better than where he lives now in that one room above the hardware store. We'll park the Hummer right next to the trailer in case of an emergency—like your car goes in the ditch or one of my hounds get loose and I got to chase 'em all over the county. But we can't let the sheriff get his hands on that vehicle or we will never see it again."

Chapter 6

Within a week, Boog was eating K-rations and freeze dried spaghetti to his heart's content. The trailer was positioned in a corner of the parking lot, and it looked like a command center with the Hummer parked conspicuously close. Sheriff Minor took immediate offense to the commissioners' directive of "Hands off" and filed a grievance with the local state congressional representative. He received a form letter back that thanked him for his concern and gave an address for any monetary support he might want to send for the representative's upcoming re-election campaign that might inspire review of his inquiry in the next general session.

Sheriff Reginald Cornwallace Minor was a four-term sheriff standing for re-election in the upcoming fall vote. He found favor with the electorate of Hinkley County by running the jail on a very low budget and attending every fund-raising barbeque in the county and every funeral of any notoriety. He always dressed in his neatly pressed sheriff's uniform, his beaver Stetson tilted just so, and maintained a steadfast dislike for any other law enforcement department that entered his domain. He tolerated petty offenses of juveniles as long as the parents were upstanding, voting, campaign-contributing citizens, and he took a drink or two when invited, despite being in uniform.

The big Hummer was like having a prickly pear thorn in the sheriff's shiny Wellington boot. Every time he walked out of the courthouse to get in his full-sized SUV, which was decked out with all the law enforcement trimmings, he had to look at that Hummer, an even bigger example of government authority, waste, and prestige. It really hurt. It hurt so much he considered impounding the vehicle and having it disappear, but he was not sure of the string of ownership and knew a federal investigation of misuse of federal property could lead to the tentacles of the state and federal prosecutorial bureaucracy infiltrating his department and potentially uncovering certain other, as Sheriff Minor put it, indiscretions necessary in the perpetual battle against crime. But he had a plan. It just needed a little fine-tuning.

•••

Boog spent his evenings reading the manuals, making hand written notations on pages of interest, digesting without comprehension the majority of the bureaucratic mumble jumble. He did note with much delight that the designated county director of homeland security had considerable power. He was automatically bestowed federal law enforcement status and was considered a deputy federal marshal with credentials available upon submission of a twenty-three-page application and a certified copy of his birth certificate. This designation allowed him to carry or operate a firearm, including automatic weapons and any moveable armament with barrel size lesser than but including fifty-caliber. Use of a weapon over fifty caliber required training and was available upon written request and completion of a twenty-page application contained within.

The red binder containing general procurement procedures, and a full-color, one-hundred-and-thirty-page outline of all available equipment was most interesting. Boog got his official Department of Homeland Security magic marker out of the desk drawer and began circling items that looked interesting. First, there was the eighteen-foot Boston Whaler search and rescue boat with a two hundred and fifty horsepower, four-stroke outboard that looked a lot like Syd Featherstone's bass boat. Only this boat had high railings around the bow, strobe emergency lights on a canvas-covered top, optional radar, sonar, grappling hooks, nitroglycerin detection kit, color-coordinated DHS life jackets, and upon completion of a special application, a bomb-sniffing canine. He put a big circle around the picture of the boat.

There was an off-road four-wheeler equipped with rifle holster, ammo box, snow blade, matching DHS helmet, and snowsuit with matching trailer. Another big circle.

Boog finished his shopping with the feeling there was no use being too greedy in this first order, even though Mister Shi-thead had made it pretty clear there was no limit when it came to homeland security. The only problem seemed to be how to place the order. He had ordered out of the Bass Pro Shop catalogue a time or two, but all you had to do was call an 800 number and talk to a nice girl who tried to sell you more than what you needed. He looked at the cover of the procurement binder and could not find an 800 number. The only identification was Department of Homeland Security, Washington DC. He did remember Marty Ringwald giving him a card as she and Shi-thead were exiting the Hummer and running for the helicopter. He had put the card in the visor of the Hummer, but Mabel had the only set of keys and specific instructions from Mister Sadinski not to let them out of her sight. Boog spent the day devising a plan, in between trips to the boiler room to scan the newest Playboy that came in a brown paper cover to County Clerk Steven's office every month. Since Boog picked up the mail every day, he merely pulled the package from the mail and delayed delivery until he had a chance to savor every page—twice.

Chapter 7

Once a month, Billy Bob's Commercial Vacuum Service came to the courthouse after closing, vacuumed the parking lot with his pickup-mounted commercial vacuum, and raked trash from the evergreens surrounding the building. The Hummer and trailer had been parked in the lot just after the last service and had not been moved since. Boog saw this as a perfect opportunity. As the clock hanging in the hall across from his office ticked toward four thirty, official closing time for the courthouse, he waited patiently. He knew Mabel would begin her preparation for departure at four o'clock and lock the door at exactly four-twenty-seven, leaving the three remaining minutes to get downstairs to the back door. Boog waited until four-twenty-five and nonchalantly walked into her office.

"They're vacuuming the parking lot tonight, so I'll have to move the Hummer. Mister Sadinski said he left the keys with you." The inference that Sadinski had okayed this release of the precious keys was borderline when it came right down to the facts, but it was not a lie, and Boog felt comfortable with it because he never lied.

Mabel looked down her long nose at him and then looked at the clock that had just ticked four-twenty-seven. "He didn't say anything to me about moving that damned truck or giving anyone the keys."

Tick, tick, tick, the time just kept slipping away and soon she would be working past quitting time. Tick, tick, tick, four-twenty-eight…

He let the time slide a little more, knowing how this interruption of her schedule irritated her. "I suppose you could try to track him down—I mean, to get an okay. Let's see," he made an obvious motion of his head toward the clock, "it's four-twenty-nine—oops, four-thirty. I'd say he's probably at the Hinkley House Lounge or maybe at the Country Squire; it's all you can eat catfish night, you know." Tick, tick, tick. "Or we could call Billy Bob and tell him to skip it this month, but you know how Sheriff Minor gets if there's a beer can in the parking lot." Tick, tick, tick. Boog thought he saw a bead of sweat form under Mabel's nose and work its way down her mustache.

"Shit fire, why do I have to be the one to keep track of you? You damn well better be a tellin' me the truth, Booger." Mabel reached into her purse, pulled out a key ring the size of a softball, and searched for the right key. She fingered a small key on the ring and shoved it into her locked desk drawer, pulling out the Hummer keys attached to an official Department of Homeland Security key ring. She flung them at Boog, slammed the drawer shut, and yelled, "Now get out of here."

Boog, feeling great satisfaction and wearing a broad smile, walked back to his office as Mabel breezed by him, humping for the elevator, swearing under her breath with each step.

Chapter 8

Boog bided his time, waiting for the courthouse to clear and the last car to leave the parking lot. Only then did he slowly walk out the back door, allowing the familiar clank of the lock bolt to announce his exit. There in front him stood a giant yellow machine that screamed *freedom*. There was no four-wheeled road machine in the county more agile, powerful, or beautiful than the yellow Hummer that awaited his command. He pressed the remote keyless entry, the doors clicked, and the headlights flashed, as if the heart and soul of the monster had awakened and winked at him with satisfaction. He approached slowly, examining the detail of the twenty-inch alloy wheels and the chrome metal brush screens over the halogen headlamps, running his hand slowly along the curve of the chest-high fender. It is a monster, he thought. A monster waiting to be tamed, subdued, and put to work protecting Hinkley County from the forces of evil that would subvert what our forefathers fought and died for, to repeat a phrase from Mister Shi-thead's speech. The keys in Boog's hand put him in control of the monster's power.

He opened the door and once again stepped into the cockpit, admiring the numerous dials and controls, sensing the transfer of power as he gripped the steering wheel. He reached up, retrieved Marty's card from the visor, and stared at her name, embossed in gold, simple and direct: Marty Ringwald, Assistant to the Assistant Undersecretary of the Department of Homeland Security. Under it was a toll-free number and a cell number. He admired the card, raised it to his nose, and sniffed, just in case there was a lingering scent, but the only odor he caught was the indescribable smell of a newly manufactured car, which in itself was a pleasing aroma.

Inserting the key into the ignition port brought the dials and twinkling dash lights to life. Numerous warnings flashed as the computer did diagnostics in preparation for the actual ignition of the motor. The door locks clanked shut and a digital readout displayed "Exterior Security Activated." Another digital screen displayed "Input Your Height and Weight" and provided spacing for the keyboard input. Boog digested the command and gave lengthy thought to the need for such information. On his last short excursion from the school lot, he had merely taken over the seat after Shi-thead ran for the helicopter. Not wanting to offend the monster, he punched the keyboard with what he guessed to be accurate data. As soon as he hit enter after the final input, his seat began to self-adjust and the foot pedals moved, putting him in perfect alignment with the steering wheel and controls. All that was left now was to turn the key and start the gigantic engine. He thought it couldn't hurt to just hear the engine run one more time, to feel the power pulse through the steering wheel into his hands, to feel the vibration in the seat and maybe even take a little spin around the parking lot. Boog grinned with delight. The head of the Hinkley County Department of Homeland Security was ready to roll, ready to take on any emergency or person that threatened the security of the fine people of Hinkley County. All was good with the world for about ten seconds as he reached down to turn the key, then Sheriff Minor pulled into the parking lot and parked in front of the Hummer. The windows of Minor's SUV were tinted, as were the windows of the Hummer, so Boog could not tell if the sheriff was watching him, but he still slowly slumped down in the seat as low as possible.

Sheriff Minor opened his door and stepped out of the SUV, positioning his Stetson, brushing any wrinkles out of his pants, hiking his belt and miscellaneous attached equipment, cracking numerous knuckles as he surveyed the scene and slowly walked toward the Hummer. He stopped, took in the menacing presence of the machine, and then proceeded to walk around it, no doubt admiring with some jealousy the intimidating size in comparison to his own vehicle. Boog realized that with the dark tinted windows, Sheriff Minor could not see if anyone was in the driver's seat. The sheriff never carried a weapon on his belt so there was no immediate threat of being shot, but Boog's stomach was knotted up in apprehension as Sheriff Minor inspected his motorized competition.

Boog decided he had better step out and try to explain what he was doing, figuring the explanation he gave Miss Hinkley would suffice. Sheriff Minor was slowly coming around the back of the Hummer on the driver's side, admiring each detail, when Boog opened the door.

Sheriff Minor gasped and jumped back, losing his hat, and almost fell down, retrieving his balance at the last second and grabbing his chest with an agonizing groan. "Boog, what the he-ell do you think you're doing? You crazy som-bitch, you about gave me a heart attack." The sheriff was still gasping for breath, bent over with one hand on his thigh and the other on his heart. "What you doin' in that truck?"

"I—I was just getting ready to move the Hummer so Billy Bob could vacuum the lot tonight. Then you pulled in, and—well, here I am."

Minor adjusted his hat, brushed imaginary dirt off his shirt-sleeves, gained a little composure and said, "Where'd you get the keys?"

"Miss Hinkley gave them to me so I could move the—"

"Yeah, yeah, I know. Billy Bob's vacuum. You drive this thing yet?" Minor asked, getting a little closer to see inside.

"Just back from the schoolhouse," Boog said, still sitting in the driver's seat.

"Scoot over. Let me get a look at this thing."

Boog pulled himself over the broad center console into the passenger's seat and Sheriff Minor took the driver's position. The digital screen reported "New Driver Detected. Input Your Height and Weight." Sheriff Minor looked at Boog, and Boog said, "Just punch those buttons with your height and weight, and it will adjust the seat."

"Well I'll be dipped," Sheriff Minor said, punching in some data. The seat and pedals moved simultaneously, and the sheriff smiled. "This is some kind o' truck, ain't it, Boog? Som bitch has a mind of its own. Let's take her for a little test drive." He turned the key, and the engine roared to life, the sound amplified by the metal passenger enclosure. Information poured across the digital screens, announcing oil pressure, tire pressure, length to next non-moving object, longitude and latitude coordinates with a complete street map and an ominous red blinking light marking the position of the vehicle on the map. The dark tinted windows gave the passengers a sensation of being inside the cockpit of an airliner preparing for takeoff. And takeoff they did. Sheriff Minor put the vehicle in gear and punched the gas petal, his white knuckles grasping the wheel and maneuvering around his SUV into the public street.

Boog held on as best he could and said, "Uh, I don't know if this is a good idea. Mister Sadinski said no one was supposed to drive this thing unless he said it was all right."

All Sheriff Minor said was, "Screw him," as he raced down Main Street making a sharp turn, wheels screeching, nearly running over an old couple waiting for the light to turn green in a 1965 Ford Falcon. Boog could see the horror in the couple's eyes as the Hummer raced by, Sheriff Minor braking and accelerating at the same time causing the vehicle to strain and shimmy, all four wheels grabbing for traction.

"Better turn on the flashing lights, Boog, I need all the room I can get to keep this monster under control." Boog searched for the correct toggle switch to turn on the strobe emergency lights while using one hand to stay upright. He found the correct switch, and the button that controlled the siren as well. The whoop, whoop of the siren cleared the street as they swerved through traffic heading out of town. The digital speedometer read seventy-plus miles an hour, and the sheriff wore a broad smile as he laid waste to the asphalt.

"Let's see what this baby will do off-road." He jerked the wheel, and they swerved off the paved surface, leaping through a ditch and heading across a freshly plowed field being prepared for winter wheat. Mud flew as they did donuts in the plowed field, hurled through a drainage ditch, and decimated a fence-row, leaving barbed wire affixed to the front bumper and a fence post trailing behind the truck. They bounced back up on the hard pack with the sheriff gut laughing and slapping the steering wheel as they headed back toward town. "Damn, this is one fine piece of machinery. No wonder we're kicking ass in I-rack. Put a machine gun on top of this baby, and I'd put a stop to all this immigration nonsense, too."

The sheriff was quiet for a few minutes then regained his serious law enforcement demeanor and said, "The damn commissioners won't give me the keys, you know. Say this here is a political appointment, this homeland security thing. Say, you are the director, that right?"

Boog was looking out of the window, acting as if he was not listening. "Oh, you mean me? Well, they did say I am supposed to take care of this truck, keep it clean and such. And I can live in the trailer. And Mister Shi-thead said the county needed a director. So I guess that's why they—well, you know, made me the director. So's there'd be one, I guess."

"Who's this Sh-whatever. Who's he?"

Boog acted as if he'd sneezed and pulled the card out of his pocket. He glanced at it and responded, "He's the assistant undersecretary of the Department of Homeland Security and Emergency Management Agency and head of procurement for the Midwest Region, and his assistant is the assistant to the assistant undersecretary of the Department of Homeland Security. And I'm the director that's under the assistant to the assistant undersecretary of the Department—"

"Okay, I get the picture, Boog," Sheriff Minor interrupted. He continued as if talking to himself. "So, they made you director. Think they can horse everyone around, play this little game with the feds. Probably hoping everyone will forget and Sadinski will put this little number in his barn next to that damn tractor. Then put the trailer at his place at Lake Ochomeechee.

Ever been there, Boog? Nice place, real quiet, great fishing." Boog opened his mouth to answer but the sheriff didn't give him a chance. "Director, huh? Well, I'll tell you what, Boog. I'm going to make you a special deputy. That's right. Hold up your right hand. No, Boog, the right one—over there. Do you solemnly swear to believe in God, uphold the Constitution of the United States, hate commies and ragheads, do whatever you are told by the sheriff of this county and…and keep me informed about this homeland security business? If so, say, 'I do.'"

Boog looked at his right hand and at the sheriff. "I do, I guess."

"There ain't no guessin' about it, Boog; you either do or you don't. This ain't no guessin' game. I'm making you a deputy, I mean special deputy, with special powers. That means when I need you, I want you coming, lickity-split—with this truck, you understand? No checking with Sadinski or Featherstone—just come, lights a-flashin' and si-reen a-blarin'. Got it, Special Deputy Boog?"

"Yes, sir."

"That's what I like to hear." They pulled into the parking lot and parked, still dragging the fence post. "Get this thing cleaned up and ready for a real emergency, Special Deputy Boog." Sheriff Minor stepped from the Hummer and walked toward his SUV, stopping and looking back at Boog, who was trying to dislodge the barbed wire from the brush bar and front bumper. "And don't give those keys back. They ask you about the keys, you just tell them you are now a special deputy and under my direct orders." Sheriff Minor turned back toward his SUV, still talking. "Those silly bastards want to play with the big boys? They better step out of their dresses and come to the back of the barn."

Chapter 9

Boog was sitting at his desk, holding Marty's card, waiting for the clock to strike nine AM, anticipating calling her. He wasn't sure yet what he would ask other than how his recent order from the federal catalogue was going, but knew he wanted to hear her voice again. He had inadvertently stumbled upon an official procurement form while looking through the manuals and placed an order using the commissioners' facsimile machine.

Mabel stopped at his door and held out her hand. "The keys, Booger." Boog looked up and felt his throat close down and mouth go dry. He tried to speak, but only grunted a raspy reply. Mabel leaned a little closer. "What? What was that? Just give me the keys before Commissioner Sadinski gets here."

Boog swallowed, trying to wet his mouth. "Sheriff Minor, uh—" He cleared his throat. "Sheriff Minor kind of—took the keys. Or at least, took control of the keys. He told me—"

"Oh, for God's sake, Booger, why would you give him the keys? I knew it; I just knew it. I knew I should never have let you have those keys." She turned and walked down the hall, still talking. "I don't know why I'm the one has to watch out for Booger. It was never my job before. I don't get paid enough for this."

Boog heard the door slam shut, and he hurried out of his office and downstairs to the information desk. As usual, Stella was off gathering gossip, so the switchboard was unattended. He picked up the handset and dialed the toll-free number from the card and heard the dainty voice he remembered so clearly say, "Office of the Assistant Undersecretary of Homeland Security—may I help you?"

"Yeah—I mean, yes—this is Boo—Jasper Simpson from Hinkley County. You brought me a Hummer last month. Well, you and Mister Shi-thead, you remember?"

"Jasper, how nice to hear from you. I'm so glad you called. I received your requisition for the boat and the four-wheeler.

They are our most popular items. Now, the crossbow and the tree stand, I haven't seen those ordered before, but most of our directors are from the big cities and I suppose there are different ways of staking out a terrorist hideout and such. I also received your application for the deputy federal marshal credentials and badge, and it will be sent overnight to you tomorrow. Your application was kind of, well, lacking in background information, and the FBI called, but Assistant Undersecretary Shi-thead gave you a glowing recommendation, and they agreed to forego all of the usual investigation stuff—you know, since we are in such a national crisis and all. So, how is everything going? Any problems that I can help with?"

Boog was just listening to the rhythm of her voice and thinking about her aroma. He kept thinking about coconuts, but didn't understand why. When she asked him a question, he was not prepared to answer, not having much experience with female social intercourse, or any kind of intercourse, for that matter. "Well, uh, it's going fine, I guess. The sheriff made me a special deputy."

"Jasper, not to step on your sheriff's toes or anything, but as a deputy federal marshal, you will have superior jurisdictional authority over the county sheriff. Assuming there are no other federal authorities in the county, like an FBI office or something, you will be the highest-ranking civil law enforcement officer in the county, probably anywhere within one hundred miles. Now, granted, he probably won't accept that fact—most of them don't—but facts are facts, and federal anything trumps state or county anything. Just remember that. You are an important cog in the mechanism necessary to fight radical factions trying to overthrow our government. You are our eyes and ears in Hinkley County. The president is counting on you."

"What president?" Boog asked meekly.

"The big guy, White House, Washington DC, the commander and chief—you know. He is the one that set this whole system up after 9/11. The whole idea is to make everyone cognizant of the evil that lurks all around us, for everyone to pay attention, watch their neighbors and anyone that looks suspicious, to pay attention to the little things that may lead to another big attack. And Jasper, in the little time we were together, I must say, I know you are just the person for this job. I could tell from the moment you helped me with the door that you are the kind of person that takes charge."

"Yeah, well, I guess I do, sometimes," Boog said, trying to remember why he called.

"Jasper Simpson, you are a true American hero, one of the good people, just remember that. I have to go now. Remember, you are on the front lines, and I am here to support you any way I can. Just call." The line disconnected, and he continued to hold the phone to his ear, wondering why the president would care about someone in Hinkley County.

He sat the phone down and turned to face Chet Sadinski, standing with his arms crossed, hat tilted just right and a stern look on his face. "Where are the keys, Boog?"

"I, well, the sheriff, uh—"

"The sheriff has the keys now? That sleazy lizard bastard, I knew he would be sticking his nose in this. Smells money, that's what he does. I don't know what this county is coming to; you can't trust anyone anymore, not even the law. Did he put you up to this?" Boog started to answer, but didn't have the chance. "This changes everything. Wait until we start the budget hearings next month. I'll cut his budget so much he'll have to use his own inmates for patrol. He wants to play the game this way, that's fine; I can play dirty, too." Sadinski turned and walked down the hall. "This isn't over yet," he said, entering the elevator.

Chapter 10

Boog sat in his office, staring at Marty's card, reenacting the telephone conversation, and thinking about what he should have said. Stella stuck her head in the door and said, "Sheriff called. Wants you to go over to the school and clean up the lab. Said the principal called and blabbered on about a thermometer or something. Take a mop and bucket." She stepped back into the hall and then hesitated, turning back, facing him. "And Boog, the ladies' restroom could use some attention downstairs. I know you are some kind of big shot now, but somebody has to clean the toilets. Anyway, you better bust your butt over to the school. You know how the sheriff is."

Boog reached under his desk drawer and pulled the set of keys to the Hummer away from the underside of the drawer where he had taped them. No need to take a mop and bucket; the school has plenty of them, he thought. He made his way out to the Hummer, smiling to himself, realizing he was now officially in control of the vehicle and a special deputy sheriff as well. He unlocked the Hummer and sat down in the driver's seat. The digital readout immediately displayed "Driver Number One" and the seat and pedals adjusted to his setting. He flipped on the emergency strobe lights and headed for the school.

Turning the corner at the school, he found the entire student body standing in the parking lot with teachers and administrators yelling and maneuvering to keep everyone orderly and in groups. Boog pulled up to the front door, stepped out, and found Principal Smithy standing on the steps.

"Boog, what are you doing here? Where's the sheriff? And where in the world did you get that thing?" Principal Smithy said, shaking his head as he pointed at the Hummer.

Principal Smithy was a pudgy man in his sixties, bald except for puffs of thin hair on both sides of his head above his ears. He was well past retirement age, but still hoping for that last promotion to a superintendent position to round out his pension. He had been principal when Boog was in high school and knew him well. He had a large round head and no visible neck. The students affectionately referred to him as Bozo behind his back.

"Boog, I don't know why you are here, but I don't have time for you right now. The first month of school and this happens. Whatever your problem is, it will have to wait. And get that truck or whatever it is out of here. It'll be in the way when the EPA gets here."

"The sheriff sent me over here. He said there was a mess in the lab." Boog was looking at the school entrance as he spoke, and when he turned around, Principal Smithy had walked away and was disciplining a student who had been throwing stones at a teacher's vehicle parked nearby.

Boog walked up the steps and entered the building. He knew exactly where the lab was located and knew there was a janitorial closet nearby. His memory served him well because the school custodian, Tug Longwater, had befriended him in high school, and he'd stayed after school many times to help Tug clean the rooms. While cleaning, Tug would reminisce about his Cherokee ancestors, who lived on the Nations before being herded further west in the middle of the nineteenth century. He learned more history from Tug than from anything taught in the classroom.

He went to the closet, retrieved a broom and some treated sawdust used to capture dust bunnies, and went to the lab. Near the back of the classroom, a small temperature thermometer was broken and lying on floor, the kind given as advertising tokens long ago. This one had a cardboard backing that said Bud's Sonoco with a scantily dressed female gas attendant holding the thermometer. Bud's Sunoco had closed soon after the Wal-Mart was built across town and started selling gasoline a dime cheaper than Bud could buy it wholesale. Boog thought, Wal-Mart would never give you a free thermometer.

The glass tube had broken, and the mercury was in a puddle on the floor. Boog looked around for any other mess, assuming there had to be something of greater significance than a broken thermometer. He found nothing, so he threw down some sawdust that absorbed the mercury, swept it all up in a small pile, and looked for somewhere to place the discard. There was a mason jar with a dead cricket in it, so Boog funneled the sawdust and broken glass into the jar, replaced the lid, and headed for the classroom exit, shutting off the light and closing the door. Stepping into the hall, he was met by three emergency personnel that had been summoned from Cougar Falls. All three had on white biosphere suits with large glass covers over their faces. The suits appeared somewhat inflated, reminding him of the Michelin Man advertising mascot, and he could hear the rattling inhale and exhale of each suit occupant breathing through exotic filtering devices. The suits had the initials EPA stenciled across the front in big letters. In front of the three was a small, four-wheeled robotic device with a mechanical arm protruding from its top. One of the suit occupants was holding a control panel in an oversized white gloved hand and appeared to be operating the mechanical arm.

A voice projected by an electronic sound reproduction system that reminded him of Darth Vader said, "Step back. We are here to remove the mercury lead hazard. Step back and you will not be harmed. Do not touch anything, and remove your shoes and clothes before leaving the building."

Boog stood motionless, looking at the suited people, and then looking at the mechanical arm. No one moved. All he heard was the inhale, exhale of the suits. Slowly, he held up the jar, pointed at it with his other hand, and then pinched his nose, the international sign of nastiness, to indicate that it contained the toxic substance. He slowly knelt down, keeping eye contact with the glass faces, and moved the glass jar within reach of the mechanical arm. Inhale, exhale, inhale, exhale—then there was a buzz, and the arm moved, awkwardly reaching for the jar with a jerking motion. At first, the clamp end of the arm grasped

Boog's wrist, missing the jar, and squeezed with enough pressure to pinch his skin. Boog grabbed the arm and pulled it off, inadvertently upsetting the robot with a crash in the otherwise silent hall. Inhale, exhale, inhale, exhale. The electronic voice said, "I hope you didn't break that; it's rented."

Boog righted the mechanical arm, and this time held it and placed the bottle in the clamshell clamp until the white suit pressed the right button and the jar was secure. Then everyone did an about-face, including the robot, and they all followed as it slowly rambled down the hall to the front door. At the front door, another white suit held a steel box with "Biohazard" stenciled on the side. The mechanical arm buzzed, raised the jar, and dropped it in the steel box. The white suit closed the steel box, twisted the hermetically sealed locking handle, sat the box down, and turned toward the crowd of on-looking students with a white-gloved thumbs-up. The crowd burst into applause, yells, and whistles. The white suit came over to Boog, put its white-suited arm around his shoulder, pointed at Boog with its white glove, and then gave another white-gloved thumbs-up. The crowd again burst into raucous applause. A photographer from the twice-weekly *Hinkley Messenger* took numerous photos of the victory celebration, and the reporter from WERM stuck a microphone up to Boog and asked, "What was it like in there, Mister Simpson, in your own words?"

Boog looked at the crowd and the microphone, opened his mouth, but nothing came out.

Principal Smithy walked up, briskly pushed the white-suited EPA person aside, put his arm around Boog, smiled at the photographer, and said, "Boog is a graduate of Hinkley High, near the top of his class, as I recall, the kind of model student this school is proud to say is one of our own. Never thought about the danger to himself, just went right in and faced the dangerous, uh, situation and took control."

The reporter switched off her recorder, satisfied with the sound bite. The photographer took one last photo and turned for his car. Principle Smithy turned around, gave the high sign, and the students began lining up and re-entering the school.

Sheriff Minor, his SUV's emergency lights flashing and engine roaring, came skidding to a halt next to the Hummer. Most of the students had reentered the building and the Environmental Protection Agency contingent from Cougar Falls was nearly loaded and ready to leave. Sheriff Minor jumped from the SUV, sensing a situation that would possibly lead to newspaper or radio coverage with him in the forefront, and hustled up to Principal Smithy.

"Damn, Jerry, you didn't tell me this was a big emergency. All you said was that a thermometer broke in the lab. What's all this EPA nonsense?" Sheriff Minor studied the remaining assemblage looking for the newspaper photographer, adjusting his hat and brushing away any unsightly wrinkles in his chinos.

"The State High School Safety Manual says that any mercury spill has to be handled as a category one emergency. We have to notify EPA, EMS, DHS, HGTV, I don't know—a whole slew of agencies. Then we have to evacuate the school. Somehow, Boog here went in and helped them clean it up, and they said he did a great job, saved all kinds of time and money the way he handled it. I suspect he'll be on the front page tomorrow. The photographer already left, if that's who you are looking for."

Sheriff Minor turned and gave a tight grin. "I'm not looking for anyone. Just making sure everyone is safe. I was in an important meeting when you called, or I would have taken care of this myself."

"Stella said you were getting a haircut," Principal Smithy said curtly. "Anyway, it's all over now." And he turned and walked up the steps into the building.

Boog stood sheepishly near the Hummer, leaning on the fender, trying to be as inconspicuous as possible. Sheriff Minor turned and gave him a hard stare. "So you saved the day. First emergency as a special deputy and you're a hero. Well, don't let it go to your head. Some deputies go their whole career without any recognition. You just got lucky. Well, it looks like this mess is cleaned up; let's go back to the funny house and see if there's any other trouble brewing in Hinkley County."

Then Sheriff Minor did something no one had ever seen him do before. He walked over to Boog and put his arm around his shoulder. "Boog, I like your style, boy. You remind me of my-self when I was younger. No bullshit, just straight fact. See a problem? You go fix it. You keep it up you might be sheriff some day. Of course, not unless I retire, or run for governor or something." He laughed and walked toward his SUV.

Chapter 11

The twice-weekly *Hinkley Messenger* came out on the Saturday following what came to be known as the great Hinkley High mercury disaster. The lead story carried a quarter-page picture of Boog with the suited EPA person giving a thumbs-up to the crowd. The story captured the seriousness of the disaster by depicting Boog, the director of the Hinkley County Department of Homeland Security and Emergency Management Agency, as the first responder, with a smaller picture of the Hummer with its DHS insignia. The article's author was Red Redderson, and it reported as follows:

Toxic Scare at Hinkley High

Hinkley High School suffered a near miss Thursday when a substantial amount of toxic mercury lead was spilled in the biology lab. A source within the school that chose not to be identified said the spill consisted of a quart jar of mercury. According to the National Center for Disease Control, that was enough mercury to poison the water supply of a major metropolitan community. At press time, it was unknown how that much mercury could have gotten into the biology lab, but school officials had not yet concluded their investigation. An undisclosed source said that it may have come from the now-defunct Bud's Sunoco, but since the owner, Bud Bonnano, died over a year ago and his closest surviving relative refused to be interviewed, the origin of the mercury could not be confirmed. The first emergency responder to the scene was Jasper Simpson, the new director of the County Department of Homeland Security and Emergency Management. It has also been confirmed that Sheriff Reginald Minor had recently appointed Jasper Simpson as special sheriff deputy of Hinkley County to complement his promotion to director of the new department.

Principal Jerry Smithy said, "Jasper Simpson, an honored graduate of Hinkley High and potential hall of fame honoree, entered the school, secured the disaster scene, and single-handedly, without concern for his own well being, contained the mercury for disposal by the Environmental Protection Agency personnel dispatched from Cougar Falls." A spokesperson for the Department of Homeland Security identified as the assistant to the assistant undersecretary of the Department of Homeland Security advised they had no knowledge of the disaster in Hinkley County but would pass the information to the assistant to the assistant undersecretary of the Federal Emergency Management Agency (FEMA) for possible emergency low interest loans for everyone directly or indirectly affected by the disaster. Those interested should contact the office direct or go on line (www.freegovernmentdisastermoney.gov) and file for immediate cash relief. In addition, the assistant undersecretary of the Department of Homeland Security will file for a special commendation from the president of the United States for Jasper Simpson for action above and beyond the call of duty by saving the county from potential harm and loss of life by mercury poisoning. The spokesperson went on to say they were very aware of Jasper Simpson's work organizing Hinkley County's department and were cognizant of his exceptional skill and abilities. Mr. Simpson has recently been appointed deputy federal marshal for the Central States territory and will have jurisdiction over a large area, including but not limited to, Hinkley County.

Boog was cleaning the ladies' room toilets Monday morning, whistling to himself, thinking about going to the boiler room when he finished and relaxing for an hour looking at the new Playboy again, when he noticed considerable noise coming from the courthouse lobby. His regular routine brought him to the building at least an hour before the doors opened for public access, and glancing at his watch, he noted that it was about time for all of the offices to fill with employees, but it was unusual for any commotion this early in the lobby. Stella didn't even start answering the phone for another fifteen minutes. He had the scrub bucket holding the door open and peeked out. Several people were milling around the lobby, two of them on ladders hoisting a banner that spread between two floor-to-ceiling columns. He could not see what was on the banner, but he assumed it was advertising some fund-raising event scheduled in the near future. Boog finished cleaning, pushed the bucket and mop outside into the lobby, and leaned against the handle, watching the group talk. A box of donuts was on a portable table, along with a coffee pot and disposable cups. Boog leaned the broom against the wall and nonchalantly walked toward the table, assuming that, as usual, no one would take notice of him, and if they did, he was prepared to answer in the affirmative that, yes, he had just washed his hands and would use the plastic tongs when reaching for a donut.

He used the tongs to secure a cake donut with multi-colored sprinkles on top, his favorite, and turned to observe the continuing commotion. In the corner of the lobby, adjacent to the banner, was a large picture sitting on an easel. The picture was of a white suit, like that he had seen at the high school, posing with another person. Boog took a bite of his donut and moved closer to get a better look, straining to see the face in the picture. One of the people in the lobby saw him and yelled, "Here he is."

Everyone turned and began clapping their hands. Boog turned and looked over his shoulder in the direction everyone seemed to be looking, wondering who had entered the room. Stella bounced from the receptionist's desk and hurried over to Boog, hugging him and pushing him toward the middle of the room. Everyone gathered around, slapping him on the back and congratulating him for a job well done.

Boog said, "It ain't that clean yet. I still have to mop and empty the trash container."

The remark caused a pause in the celebration and then Stella said, "Boog, we don't care about the toilets; you're a celebrity. Haven't you seen the paper? You're a hero. You saved the day at Hinkley High. Nobody around here has gotten this much attention since Commissioner Bellows was arrested by the highway patrol for riding his horse down Main Street drunk. The paper said you might even get a call from the president."

"What president?" Boog asked, waiting for the punch line or for someone to yell, "Gotcha!"

"What president?" Stella said, mimicking Boog. "The president of our United States. The one and only. The paper said you might get some kind of prize for what you done."

The rest of the crowd kept saying, "Yeah, Boog," and "Way to go, Boog," and "You the man, Boog."

All Boog could think of was the fake rat in the toilet. Someone had gone to a lot of trouble to make fun of him again, and he wasn't going to fall for it. Then Commissioner Sadinski walked in the front door, looked up at the banner that proclaimed Jasper Simpson, American Hero, looked at the enlarged photograph of Boog and the white suit, surveyed the group of congratulatory revelers, and said, "Ain't you people got anything better to do? This ain't no party barn; it's the damn county courthouse, and the people of Hinkley County aren't paying all these salaries just so you can dance around and pat each other on the back." He scowled as he looked from one person to the other and eventually landed on Boog. "And you—you're fired." And with his grand entrance complete, he turned and walked toward the elevator.

At least now, Boog knew it wasn't a joke.

Everyone was mumbling, and someone hastily climbed the ladder to take down the banner, remove the photograph, and get rid of the donuts.

Stella put her arm around Boog and consoled him. "Sorry, Boog, you did a great thing and that jerk is jealous. Everyone except him and apparently a majority of the voting public knows he's an ass."

Boog said, "I don't get it. What did I do now? First, someone says I'm a hero, and then I get fired. It don't seem right."

Stella stood contemplating, smiled, and said, "Boog, don't worry, I think I know how to handle this. Stay right here." She went to the receptionist's desk, fumbled with the phone book, and made a call. She talked, waving her hand, pointing to the banner and then to the elevator, used a couple of expletives Boog had never heard a lady use before, and hung up the phone. She came back over and said, "Just sit tight for a little while. I think Sadinski might change his mind and come looking for you."

• • •

Sadinski stormed into the commissioners' office and slammed the hall door. Mabel was used to his foul disposition, paid no attention, and said, "I'm sure you saw Saturday's paper. That was quite a story. Boog, a hero—now isn't that something?"

Sadinski turned an even brighter red, stared at Mabel for a long minute, entered the inner office, and slammed the door hard enough to knock Mabel's State Association of Commissioners' Secretaries, secretary of the year plaque off the wall.

As soon as Sadinski sat down, his phone rang, and Stella said in a casual tone, "Call for you, Mister Sadinski. The caller would not identify himself."

Sadinski pressed the blinking button, tried to calm himself in preparation for a constituent's inquiry, and said politely, "Commissioner Sadinski here."

"Commissioner Sadinski, this is Red Redderson, over at the *Messenger*. Just wanted to get your comments regarding Jasper Simpson, your new director. He made quite a stir at the school. I'm sure you saw Saturday's edition. We are doing a follow-up story. Would you mind? It will only take a minute or two." There was silence on the line. "Commissioner, you still there?"

"Yeah, I'm here," he responded with reservation.

"Okay then, just a couple questions. You must be pleased with your selection of Mister Simpson now that he has attracted so much attention with his prompt action at the school. Any comment?" Still more silence. "Still there, Commissioner?"

"Yeah, I'm here. Yeah, I'm pleased," Sadinski said curtly.

"Okay then, I can quote you on that? Yeah, I'm pleased," Red said, slowly, as if he was writing it down.

"Don't be a smart ass, okay? I'm not finished. Boog—I mean Simpson—did his job. I mean, he did a good job. Hell, he's a janitor; he should know how to clean stuff up. Wait a minute; don't write that down, that's off the record."

"What's off the record?"

"What I just said about him being a janitor."

"Well, is he a janitor?" Red was enjoying this. Sadinski was an easy mark when it came to stupid comments.

"No, goddamn it; he's, well, he's—"

"The director of Homeland Security and Emergency Management for Hinkley County?"

"Well, yeah, sort of."

"What do you mean, sort of?"

"I don't mean sort of."

"That's what you said—sort of."

"Goddamn it, don't put words in my mouth. I didn't mean sort of; I meant, yeah, he's the director, under our supervision—mine and the other commissioners'."

"And now I understand he's a deputy sheriff. Is that right?" Another long silence. "You still there?"

"You'll have to talk to the sheriff about that. He wants to appoint a bunch of people deputies. Well, I guess that's his business as long as he doesn't ask for more money."

"And our sources say he has been appointed deputy federal marshal. Are you aware of that?" There was another pause. "You—"

"Yes, I'm still here. I guess you'll have to talk to the feds about that, too. As long as Boog does what I, what we, tell him to do, I don't care what they make him."

"One last question, Commissioner. A source that wishes to remain anonymous has said, and I quote, 'Commissioner Sadinski fired Jasper Simpson this morning in front of several county employees. He didn't specify why, but he was clear about what he said. He clearly said Boog was fired.' Any comment on that, Commissioner?" Another long silence. "Still there, Commissioner?" Red asked, almost bursting trying to withhold laughter.

Sadinski now knew what this call was about. "I did not fire him," Sadinski said, slowly emphasizing each syllable. "Some of the employees were having a surprise party for Jasper in the lobby. We're kind of like a family around here, you know, and in jest—you hear that? In jest—I yelled at Boog that he was fired, just clowning around. Hell, with all the noise, I'm surprised anyone heard it." Stella, Sadinski thought to himself. It was definitely Stella that called Redderson. "Anything else?" he said cordially.

Chapter 12

Boog sat in the trailer, despondent, trying to rationalize the morning's events. After over fifteen years of working for the county, he had lost his job, and he didn't even know why. There was an almost unnoticeable knock on the trailer door. Stella was standing outside when Boog peeked out.

"Boog, Commissioner Sadinski is looking for you. I think he may have reconsidered. He came down to the lobby looking for you. His mood has changed a whole lot." Stella signaled for Boog to come out of the trailer. "Come on; let's go find him before he changes his mind again."

They walked into the rear of the courthouse and slowly made their way to the lobby, Boog apprehensive and tagging along behind Stella. Sadinski was leaning against the information counter, staring at them as they turned the corner into the lobby. Stella stopped and said, "Oops, I have to use the ladies' room," and ducked into the restroom.

"Boog, come over here," Sadinski said in a complacent tone.

Boog slowly walked toward him, taking his time, and looking around the room for potential witnesses.

"Look, Boog, maybe you didn't understand what I said this morning. I was just kidding, you know, like I do. I'm sorry if I hurt your feelings." Sadinski kept looking around the room while he talked; obviously not pleased with the position he was in. "It was just a joke. All those people laughing and joking, and I thought, you know, I would joke along with them. When I said you were fired, I was joking about you being the janitor—you know, that you were fired from being the janitor, now that you are the director of security or whatever." Sadinski felt perspiration gathering on his brow and again looked around the lobby for anyone listening. Apologizing to Boog was not something he wanted in the public domain.

Stella had the ladies' room door cracked open and was listening. She raised her fist and whispered, "Yes."

Boog said, "You mean you don't want me to clean the building anymore? Who's gonna do it?"

Sadinski tapped his fingers on the counter with one hand, ran his fingers through his hair with the other, and said, "I don't know, Boog; this is just gettin' too damn complicated. Now you just go about whatever you were doing and forget about what I said this morning. It's just too damn complicated." And with that, he turned, put his hat back on his head with force, took another look around the lobby, and exited the courthouse.

Stella came out of the ladies' room and hugged Boog again. "I told you. I knew he would back down as soon as he found out it would be in the paper."

"What about the paper?" Boog asked.

"Oh, never mind; let's get that banner back up. Boog, I'm so proud of you," Stella said, smiling and taking his hand and leading him over to the stepladder.

• • •

Two weeks later, Boog received, via the United States Post Office, a manila envelope tucked between two catalogues and accompanied by three credit card solicitations. Stella now brought the mail everyday to the commissioners' office and ever since the great Hinkley High mercury disaster, stopped at Boog's office, smiled, and personally gave him his mail, but only after she reviewed each item as if she were his personal secretary.

"Hey, Boog."

"Hey, Stell."

"You got an envelope from Washington, see it?" Stella was on her tiptoes looking over Boog's hands as he studied the items. "What do you think it is? I bet it's some kind of medal or something, like a purple heart or something. You gonna open it?"

Boog held the envelope in his hand and then held it up to the light bulb hanging from the ceiling, but the paper was too heavy to reveal anything. "Could be a letter, I suppose. The return address is Sixteen-hundred Pennsylvania Avenue. Sounds like it might be near the railroad tracks or something. Like in Monopoly—the Pennsylvania Railroad." Boog studied the envelope some more, holding it close to his face and studying the type.

"Jeez, Boog, open the damn thing. You gonna sit and look at it all day? Jeez, you're about the slowest thing I've ever seen. I'm about to wet my pants and you sit there like it's nothing." Stella was about the same age as Boog, and they had gone to Hinkley High at the same time, but they had never socialized, or even talked to one another during their entire high school career. Stella had been a cheerleader and after a Friday night indiscretion, had married one of the stellar football players a week after graduation, forfeiting her opportunity to attend college. When she divorced and took the job as the courthouse switchboard operator (for which she didn't have to apply or go through an interview process because she was Ralph Bellow's second wife's sister's daughter), she had occasionally talked to Boog, but it was mostly to ask him to clean something or pick up supplies. Since the great Hinkley High mercury disaster, Stella had taken a real interest in him, constantly finding excuses to come to the commissioners' office on the third floor and casually making conversation as she passed his office. And of course, each day she brought the mail and stuck around to see the contents of anything of perceived importance.

Boog slowly took out his pocketknife and carefully sliced the crease on the end of the envelope. Once open, he peered inside, still not pulling out the contents. "Looks like a picture of some sort."

Stella couldn't wait anymore, and grabbed the envelope from his hand and pulled out the contents. "It's a letter and a picture." Stella read aloud, "From the Office of the President of the United States. Dear Jasper Simpson—" The Jasper Simpson part had been superimposed on the form letter, not perfectly, but good enough to impress most recipients. “In appreciation for me-ritor-ious—damn, that’s a big word—service to your country, and for conducting yourself in a manner beyond the call of duty, it is my honor to recognize you for your ex-emp-lary—man, you need to be a college graduate just to read this thing—exemplary character and dedication to the fundamental freedoms that make our country the greatest nation in the world. We thank you. You are a great American. God bless us all. And it’s signed by the president, Boog, and wait, there’s more. PS: Thank you for your generous contribution helping us to continue our important work. We count on people such as yourself to help us fight for our continued freedom.” Stella moved the letter to reveal a picture of the president and his wife sitting on a porch swing, smiling like it was Christmas morning at the Rockefellers’. “The picture is signed, too, Boog. Damn, I’ve never known anyone that got a letter from the president of the United States.” Stella plopped right down on the desk, reached over, and gave Boog a big mushy kiss on the lips. “Booger, you’re really something. Who would have ever guessed?”

Chapter 13

The fall wind swirled downed leaves in the many alcoves of the courthouse building, and the shortened daylight hours brought dusky shadows early in the evening. Friday night football fever was in the air and the courthouse employees wasted no time exiting the parking lot in preparation for a crisp fall weekend. As usual, Boog was the last to leave the building and walked to his trailer, ready to endure his usual weekend routine of freeze-dried food, snacks, and television. The DHS trailer came equipped with satellite television, satellite radio, and a prepaid cell phone that, so far, Boog had not touched. It had taken him several weeks of intense concentration, reading the instruction manual, to get the electronic television receiver to work. He had to mount a small dish on top of the trailer and through trial and error find the appropriate direction to receive the signal. Once that was accomplished, the plasma TV mounted on the wall of the trailer provided a high-definition picture he had never before experienced. With the dish, he could receive almost one thousand channels of programming, some forty-seven different channels showing the same World soccer playoffs in fourteen different languages. Unfortunately, with all the technology, the local station in Cougar Falls was not available unless you had a rabbit ear antenna, which he did not.

The trailer was kept clean and orderly, something Boog was proud of, having taken seriously Tug Longwater's admonition that having a clean spirit required living a clean and orderly life. Those that could not control their surroundings could not control their own life. Success was not determined by accumulation of possessions but by clarity of thinking and cleansing of the soul through righteous living.

Boog had never known his father, and his mother died of hepatitis when he was eight. His grandparents on his mother's side raised him, but a strong father figure was never present. His grandfather considered him a financial burden and paid him little attention, thus Boog sought out any adult that showed interest or would accommodate his questions and inquiries. Tug Longwater was patient and understanding. He noticed Boog's isolation from the other children, his backward tendencies, and his lack of social interaction, something the trained counselors employed by the school failed to recognize. Tug enjoyed talking to Boog, arousing his interest in the ways of the Ancients, and on numerous occasions, invited Boog to his home for Sunday dinner. Tug died soon after Boog's graduation, and he carried the loss for many years, Tug's memories being one of the few possessions he cherished.

It was near nine o'clock, and Boog was half-asleep, watching an Australian lacrosse match on channel eight hundred and thirty-seven. He was amazed at what they could do with those little sticks with baskets on the end. There was a light knock on the door, an unusual, almost non-existent occurrence, and he wasn't sure it wasn't just leaves slapping the door's surface. There was another knock, this time with greater intensity, and a voice accompanying the knock.

"Boog, you in there?" It was a female voice—familiar, but still unrecognizable.

Boog cautiously went to the door, pulled the latch, and peeked through the crack.

"Open the damn door, Boog; it's freezing out here."

It was Stella, outfitted in a Hinkley High letter jacket, blue jeans, and running shoes. She stepped into the trailer, and Boog closed the door. She unzipped her jacket, shook her auburn hair loose, and said, "Hey, Boog."

"Hey, Stell." There was an uncomfortable moment before Stella took her jacket off, revealing her Hinkley Hornets tee shirt, and plopped down on the couch as if this was an everyday occurrence.

"What'cha doing?" she said, grabbing the remote. "What the heck kind of game is that? Neat TV, Boog; did you buy it? I was at the game, but the mighty Hornets are losing by, I don't know, thirty points or some such nonsense, so I thought, 'Why not go see what Boog is doing?'"

He was still standing at the door with his hand on the latch.

"You expecting someone else? Why are you still standing at the door?"

He pulled his hand away from the latch as if it was a hot coal and took a step closer. Not sure what to do, he leaned against the wall, crossing his arms.

"Boog, don't start this backward act, like in high school. We're thirty-some years old—friends, I hope—and I'm here to see you. No big deal. Sit down; take a load off. Got anything to drink? I mean like Coke or anything?"

Boog went to the refrigerator and took out bottled water that came with the trailer. "Uh, all I have is bottled water right now. I haven't been to the store lately. Is that okay?" He walked over and handed her the water.

"Wow, I'm gonna have to come over here more often. You need a little feminine attention around here. I'll go to the store tomorrow and get you some basics—pop, stuff like that. How do you survive without Coke?" Stella looked around the trailer for the first time. "This is pretty nice, and it's so clean, nothing out of place. Wow, Boog, my husband—ex-husband—was a slob. He expected me to follow him around and clean up his messes. He was too lazy to even throw a beer can in the trash. Oh well, that period of my life is over, thank God. Hon, you can sit down anytime now. I don't bite; at least, not on the first date."

Boog started to sit down in the chair under the TV on the wall, and Stella got up and walked to the rear of the trailer, through the bathroom, and into the bedroom. She turned on the light and said, "Wow, you are a regular Betty Crocker happy homemaker aren't you? Bed's made, clothes—all four of them—hanging up; shoes, both pairs, spaced perfectly. Boog, you weren't in the army, were you? I don't remember that; of course, I don't remember much about those few years after high school when everyone else went to college and I went to the hospital to have my first." She noticed what appeared to be his wallet laying on the stand next to the bed. It was a flip-open leather bi-fold, and after checking to see if she was visible from the living room, curiosity forced her to flip it open. Pinned to one side was a silver badge with "Deputy Federal Marshal" in an arc over a miniature presidential seal. The other side had a window showing an identification card with Boog's picture, his name, badge number, and "Deputy Federal Marshal" underneath. The picture showed him dressed in his county coveralls—the same picture used on his county employee ID. Stella laid the wallet carefully back in place as if it had sacred significance, turned, and walked through the hall and back to the couch.

"Don't get me wrong; I love my kids. I don't think you have ever seen 'em, have you? Edward, Erin, and Eric. I know, don't say it—yuppie names starting with the same letter. I was caught up in the times, trying to be like the girls that got to go to college. Unfortunately, with a husband that cared more about how the Bears did on Sunday than how I did on Saturday night, it just didn't work. We had Eddy, and that was going to be it. Then after a few years went by, things started getting sticky, and instead of going to see a priest or something, we decided to have another kid—you know, thinking it would help bring us closer. So then came Erin. Well, it didn't bring us any closer. And then one night, Bud came home all beered up and decided to have his own way, and wouldn't you know it, here comes Eric. Anyway, that was it. I mean, I love my kids, but I just couldn't deal with it anymore, you know what I mean? Probably not. God, I'm talking your ear off. I'm sorry, but I just don't get to talk to anyone my age anymore, especially a man. Eddy lives with his dad now; he's sixteen, and so I don't even get to talk to him that much. It's as if all the men that stayed in this town turned into fat slobs, and everyone else split. Oh, Jesus, I didn't mean that. I mean, you're not fat, and you're definitely not a slob. Okay, I'll shut up. Show me how to work this thing." She held up the remote. He reached for it, but she pulled it back. "No, come over here so you can see, too."

An hour later, Stella was lying on the couch, her head in his lap, hanging on to his leg, breathing softly—sound asleep. They had flipped through what seemed to be hundreds of channels before deciding on a Charlie Chaplin silent movie, Stella remarking that since he had not said more than five words since she arrived, he obviously enjoyed the silence. The movie ended, and Boog moved slightly to keep his legs from becoming completely numb.

Stella, aroused by the movement, partially sat up and looked at him. "I guess I fell asleep." She laid her head on his shoulder. "It's just so nice to be with someone other than kids and mothers of other kids. It's so quiet here and comfortable. Boog, it's okay if I come back, isn't it?" He didn't say anything at first. Stella raised her head in concern. "Isn't it?"

He said, "Sure, Stell, it's nice to have someone to talk to."

"You mean listen to. You hardly said anything all night. Speaking of all night, what time is it?" Stella looked around for a clock. He raised his arm and showed her his watch.

"Twelve-thirty; it's officially Saturday," he said.

"Damn, I've got to get home. My mother is watching the kids, and I told her I'd be home after the game. She'll go through the roof." Stella reached over and kissed him, pulled away, and then came back, putting her arms around his neck and straddling his lap. This time, she kissed him with passion and hugged him again, looking in his eyes, almost nose to nose. "I get the feeling you like that; I mean, I'm really getting the feeling," she said squirming in his lap. "Can I come back, Boog? Do you really want me to come back?"

He gulped, drew in a big breath, and said, "I would very much like you to come back."

Chapter 14

The Hinkley Harvest Fest was a weekend event held every October in the park adjacent to the high school, conveniently preceding the fall election, giving savvy politicians the opportunity to mingle with their constituents in a timely fashion. A Saturday parade opened the event with numerous floats, fire trucks, the Hinkley High marching band, and the Hinkley County Horse and Bridle Synchronized Sidestepping Stallions Club, all organized into a procession at the Super Value parking lot. The parade was scheduled to proceed up Main Street and finally disassemble in the park. Leading the parade was the Hummer, pulling a float that would carry the three commissioners. The float, reminiscent of a Roman chariot, but with four wheels, was really a farm wagon with multi-colored crepe paper decorating a railing and three velvet, swiveling lounge chairs mounted in succession. Boog sat in the Hummer, first in line, listening to the WERM morning announcer give status reports on the parade and hype Fred Ribley's Ford dealership, affectionately known locally as Fred's Fords. In between the announcements, the station occasionally played country classics, which was a pleasing diversion for Boog. The past few weeks had brought a pivotal change to his life. He had gone from a nondescript janitor living in a room above Hanover's Hardware to a well-known and recognized member of the governing infrastructure of the county. In addition, an attractive coworker was wooing him, and much to his own surprise, he was handling the attention with ease and caution. Stella had become a good friend, caring about his appearance given his new position, and adding a feminine touch to his trailer, including some flowered towels—replacing the hand rags he had confiscated from the courthouse—and fresh bed linens, replacing those provided by the manufacturer of the trailer. Scented candles were now dispersed on conspicuous shelves and the refrigerator was stocked with Coke, canned juice, and other basic essentials. Stella infrequently visited him at the trailer to watch a movie or just talk, but she had not pushed herself on him or made any uncomfortable advances. They saw each other daily in the courthouse, smiled and exchanged cordialities, opened the mail and discussed the latest gossip. She was a friend such as he had not experienced since the loss of Tug Longwater.

Sheriff Minor came strolling across the parking lot, Boog noticing him from some distance as he stopped to talk to people, shake hands, and slap backs. He eventually made his way to the Hummer and put his arm on the open passenger window, still looking at the assemblage, playing with a toothpick in the corner of his mouth. "How you doin', Special Deputy Boog, sittin' here in this fancy vehicle, gettin' ready to lead the big parade?"

As usual, Boog was at a loss for words. Minor opened the door and hoisted himself into the seat, leisurely dangling his feet outside. "It's a beautiful day for a parade, don't you think? The boys have my horse all combed out and ready to make the march to the park. Can't wait to get one of Hank's brats with a big gob of sauerkraut. Wash that down with a cold beer; it doesn't get any better than that, Special Deputy Boog."

Sheriff Minor's radio, conspicuously attached to his belt, squawked, and the dispatcher announced, "Attention, all mobiles—ten-thirteen on one-twenty-eight, one mile west of Old River road. Possible injury; township paramedics request assistance. All units in the area respond."

Minor grabbed his radio and responded, "This is Mobile One; all units are tied up with the parade. Where's the highway patrol?"

There was silence and then a response. "They gave negative response on this; said it was our turn."

"Those high falutin' bastards. They know the parade's about to start," Minor said, thinking for a minute. "Let's go, Boog." He yelled into the radio. "Mobile One responding. ETA ten minutes." He pulled his feet in and slammed the door. "The parade don't start for another half-hour; where's the si-reen and the flashers on this buggy?"

Boog looked at him, realizing the float was attached to the Hummer, and started to say, "But the fl—"

"God damn it, Boog—go, go, go. This is an emergency. Don't give me any of your lame-ass excuses. I said go."

Boog cranked the engine and slammed the vehicle into gear, spinning the wheels as it grabbed the pavement under the strain of the trailer. They roared out of the parking lot with the siren whooping and the lights flashing. The float rose on two wheels as they turned the corner exiting the parking lot, the lounge chairs affixed to the bed making it top heavy. Unknown to Boog or the sheriff, Ralph Bellows had climbed up on the trailer and decided to take a little rest in the rear lounge chair before the parade started. As the Hummer turned the corner out of the parking lot and summoned all of its horsepower to respond to the emergency, the crowd in the parking lot stood awestruck, pointing fingers, yelling, watching Ralph Bellows bear hug the rear lounge chair, trying not to be thrown from the float.

They raced down Main Street, noise from the siren and the engine making it difficult to communicate, but Boog yelled, "The float; it's still behind us."

"What? What float?" Sheriff Minor turned and looked out the back window. He saw the crepe paper flapping in the wind on the front chair of the float and Ralph Bellows' head sticking up above the rear chair. "What the hell? Who is that? Why didn't you tell me that thing was hooked up? Stop. Stop this thing. You trying to kill somebody?"

Just then, the radio squawked again. "Mobile One, you can stand down. The highway patrol decided they could delay lunch and respond. Must have gotten another call from someone. And sheriff, someone reported Booger Simpson is trying to kill Ralph Bellows by running all over town with him tied to the commissioners' float. You copy?"

"Uh, yeah, that's a ten-four. I'll check into it," Minor said, somewhat subdued, still staring out the back of the Hummer.

The Hummer slowed to a stop, and Sheriff Minor stepped out, adjusted his hat, stamped his feet to straighten his pant crease, and walked back to the float. Ralph Bellows was still hugging the chair with his knees buried in the seat, crying, and there was a big brown spot on the seat of his pants. "Hey, Ralph. Didn't know you were back here. We were just testing out the Hummer—seeing what she could do in an emergency. You need a lift or anything?"

Bellows sobbed and tried to extricate himself from the chair, half-falling into a kneeling position on the bed of the trailer, holding onto the railing. He opened his mouth to speak, but instead vomited down the side of the float, spotting Sheriff Minor's shiny patent leather shoes and black uniform pants.

"Aw, jeez, Ralph. Why'd you have to go and do that?"

Sheriff Minor and Boog wrestled Bellows off the trailer and into the back seat of the Hummer and slowly returned to the Super Value parking lot, the windows wide open, dropping Bellows at his car. Sheriff Minor wished him well, and told him the parade started in fifteen minutes and not to be late.

The parade started and finished as scheduled with Ralph Bellows conspicuously missing from the commissioners' float. Boog parked the Hummer near the bandstand with the float attached. It would be used as a throne for the Hinkley Harvest Fest King and Queen to be selected later in the day. Mission accomplished, he headed over to Hank's Hand-Stuffed Brats concession for lunch. Stella spotted him moving through the growing crowd and hurried over to join him.

"Hey, Boog."

"Hey, Stell."

"I heard you about killed Ralph Bellows this morning. What's that all about?" Stella put her arm through his as they slowly walked.

"It was an accident. He's all right. I suspect he's feelin' no pain about now at the Alibi Lounge. Not that he had any pain. I mean, nothin' happened to him this morning, 'cept a little ride on the float. Anyway, what are you doin'?"

"I have to judge the pie-eating contest at two and then take my kids over to my mother's. You gonna be around tonight for the dance?" Stella squeezed his arm.

"You had lunch?" Boog responded, avoiding the dance question. The thought of standing in front of a crowd of gawkers and attempting to wiggle his body in some sort of dance-like motion was frightening enough to make his empty stomach wrench, and as far as he was concerned, was down-right out of the question, even for Stella. They approached the concession stand, taking in the wafting aroma of grilled bratwurst, onions, and sauerkraut. A beer tent was next to the trailer and had already drawn a crowd. They gathered their sandwiches and iced soft drinks, and wandered to a vacant table in the beer tent.

Stella had just taken an oversized mouthful of bratwurst and was laughing, waving her hand in front of her mouth, trying to cool the sausage delight, when a large shadow spilled across the table from behind. Bud O'Reilly, her ex-husband, stood behind her, holding a large, disposable cup of beer in one hand and resting the other on the back of Stella's chair. Bud carried his two hundred-plus pounds on a six-two frame, but the years of overindulging in beer and lack of exercise had left him with a stomach that hung over his belt. He covered his thinning hair with a John Deere ball cap. His tight tee shirt gave notice of his swelling girth, and his sagging blue jeans completed the picture of a thirty-something that may not make it to middle age. "Well, looky here—the little couple out for a picnic in the park. Ain't that just darling."

Stella turned around and glared at Bud. "Real nice, Bud. Drunk, and it isn't even one o'clock in the afternoon. You may have set a new record." She started to turn back to her lunch and then said in true motherly fashion, "The kids ought to really enjoy seeing their father stumble around the park making an ass of himself." She turned back to Boog. "Unfortunately, it won't be the first time and for sure won't be the last."

Bud stood up straight, and it was obvious by the look on his face that the angry drunk syndrome was beginning to manifest itself. "What's it like, doin' it with a retard?" He turned, as if expecting applause for what he perceived as comic relief from the numerous other customers in the tent. Instead, all was quiet while some of the patrons turned away and others slowly rose from their chairs to exit.

"Bud, go away now," Stella said, emphasizing the now, still staring at her sandwich, and not looking up, her lips pursed and both hands wrapped around the bun. Boog was enjoying his sandwich, trying to keep the kraut from slipping out of the bun, not paying much attention, although Stella's change in tone made him look at her and then up at Bud.

"Hey, Bud," Boog said.

This caught Bud off-guard. He had just played his ace insult card, and Boog hadn't even caught it. He wasn't sure what to say next and then took note of the silence that seemed to have enveloped the tent, so he just turned and stomped off, spilling beer down the front of his tee shirt.

"I'm so sorry, Boog. He's an ass, a drunken ass, which is the worst kind." A tear trailed down Stella's face, and she sat her sandwich down and just stared at it.

Boog looked around and then looked at Stella. "Hey, Stell, don't worry about it. I've known Bud almost all my life, and he's been that way forever. He's harmless. Tug used to tell me when those guys bugged me at school, the ones with the biggest mouths are the biggest babies. He also told me that a man only reveals his fear if he responds with his mouth."

"Who is Tug? That your father?" Stella said, wiping the tear from her face.

"No, Tug Longwater—you remember, he was the janitor at school. He was half Cherokee. Very wise. Died a few years ago."

Stella looked bewildered. "I guess I don't remember the janitors. They were just, there—you know? Not someone you talked to—or at least not me. Is his family still around?"

"No, after Tug died, the casinos started springing up, and his wife and kids were awarded shares of the profits, I guess. They moved to Chicago and live in some big high-rise. I got a couple letters at first from Marsha, his wife—well, was his wife—but haven't heard anything for the past couple years. Anyway, great brat. Want another?"

Stella stared at Boog, and the tears started falling in earnest. She sniffed, and then her face scrunched up and she began to gasp for breath with each onslaught of tears. "God, why are you so, so, nice?" she sobbed and sniffed. "I've spent my whole life around men who only think of themselves; think women were created to be servants and baby sitters. And then you, you come along, and you are entirely different. I don't get it."

"I'm sorry." Boog couldn't think of anything else to say. He didn't understand why Stella was crying other than Bud must have upset her, but he'd left and she was still crying. He would sure like to have another brat, but he didn't want to just get up while she sobbed in her napkin.

"You are sorry? For what? For being the nicest person that I have ever met? For being caring, gentle and kind? God, what's wrong with me?" Stella got up and ran out of the tent.

Boog sat for a second, and then noticed those still sitting in the tent looking at him as if he had just squirted mustard in Stella's face. He rose slowly and methodically cleaned up the table, hesitating at first, looking at Stella's unfinished brat, but then thought better of it and threw the sandwich and the rest of the trash in the nearby barrel, put the seats back into position, and walked out of the tent without making eye contact. Something had just happened, but he was not sure what it was, or for that matter, what it meant. Anyway, he was pretty certain he wouldn't have to dance tonight.

Chapter 15

Monday afternoon, Boog was sitting in his office, perusing a catalogue of hunting gear that had arrived with the day's mail and considering calling Marty and checking on his tree stand and cross bow. After all, deer season was fast approaching, and he was looking forward to catching the last few warm days of fall in the woods. He heard the elevator chime and the clatter of feet fast approaching. Stella slid to a stop at his door, grabbing the door jam, and said, "Boog, someone called from Smith's dairy farm and said a little kid fell into the slop pond. They called the sheriff and then called the courthouse asking for the director of homeland security. That's you isn't it? Anyway, they sounded really scared, and I could hear people yelling and crying in the background. I asked who it was that called, and they just hung up. I suppose they're running back to the pond to help look for the kid. What are you going to do?"

"I don't know. They called the sheriff, right? Did he call for me?" Boog rose from his seat and climbed over the desk.

"No one else called. What are you going to do?" Stella was doing her little dance, stepping from one foot to the other in antsy anticipation, like a child that had to go to the bathroom.

"I guess I'll run out there and see if I can help. Smith's place—that's the big dairy farm out on Stillwater Road, right?" Boog reached under the desk and pulled the keys to the Hummer away from the bottom of the drawer. "I'll go out there; you call the sheriff's department and make sure they have enough information." Boog ran for the elevator with Stella right behind.

In the elevator descending to the ground floor, Stella reached over and kissed him. "Please be careful."

• • •

Boog roared out of the parking lot with the siren blaring and the lights flashing, heading north out of town toward Stillwater

Road. He had anticipated seeing other emergency vehicles headed the same direction, but so far, there were none in sight. He would probably be the last person to arrive. Thoughts of a desperate attempt to save a drowning child plowed through his head as he sped toward the Stillwater turnoff. The Smith dairy farm was just three-quarters of a mile off the hard pack and consisted of a two-hundred-cow milking operation. He had visited the farm on a school trip many years before and still remembered white buildings, the stainless steel holding tanks and the smell of the slop pond behind the barn. What a terrible place for a little child to fall.

He wheeled into the open barnyard and still saw no other emergency vehicles. Surmising they must be in back near the slop pond, he wheeled around the barn to the fenced pond. There were still no other emergency vehicles. He slid to a stop, climbed out of the vehicle, and ran to the fence. The smell was stifling. The slop pond was a cement pool about fifty feet wide by one hundred feet long, fed by a trough coming out of the milking barn. A skid loader worked from inside, pushing the cow manure into the trough and eventually into the pond. The pond supposedly had living bacteria to degrade the slop, but it smelled as if the process wasn't working. He surveyed the pond and saw a small child's shirt clinging to a fence barb and a doll baby lying near by. He could only assume this was where the child fell in the pond. But where was everyone else? Was he the first to arrive? It was time for a decision. Wait for help to arrive or begin a search for the child in the muck? There was only one answer, and he knew he had no choice. He climbed the fence and waded into the slop near the shirt. The pool was about three feet deep, reaching just above his waist. He worked around in a circle just in front of the shirt and doll. If he felt anything with his foot or leg, he reached into the slop and tried to feel. He was completely covered with cow manure.

Ronnie Smith came around the barn and walked up to the fence. "Hey, Boog. What the hell you doin'?"

Boog looked up to see Smitty. Then Bud O'Reilly came walking around the barn, raising a camera. "Smile, Boog; we want you to look real nice in the paper." Two other friends of Smith and O'Reilly came out of the cover of the barn and rested their arms on the fence.

Bud said, "Find anything in there, Boog? You know, you give new meaning to the phrase 'shit for brains,' you know that?" They all laughed, and Bud took another picture. "Well, boys, I think our work is done here. Boog, you just keep lookin' around in there. Smitty said he lost a quarter in there a couple years back. I'm sure you keep diving you'll find it. We'll let everyone back in town know they are all safe now. Our director of security has made sure there's no terrorists hiding in Smitty's shit pond." They all laughed, gave a couple high fives, and walked back around the barn.

Boog stood, waist-deep in manure and contemplated his situation. All he could think of was the fake rat in the toilet. He had never understood the satisfaction the auditor got from hearing a woman scream and watching her run out of the ladies' room. The same was true here. What satisfaction was there in scaring everyone with a child drowning in a slop pond? He got the part about him being the brunt of the joke. That was something he had lived with most of his life, and he took it with little or no animosity toward the people who dished it out. It was part of being on the lower rung, of not having parents that met the social standards that garnered respect in the community—for that matter, not having parents at all. It also didn't help being the kid that wore used clothes and lived with uncaring grandparents untrained in social graces. All of these factors contributed to his introverted personality.

He slowly pulled himself from the pond, did a brief personal inspection, had to laugh at what he saw, and began looking for a water hose.

The caption above the picture read, "False Alarm Causes Big Stink." The picture told the story—Boog waist-deep in the slop pond, his shirt and arms covered with manure. The story in the twice-weekly *Hinkley Messenger* read:

The new director of homeland security responded to what is being called a false alarm on Monday at the Smith Dairy Farm on Stillwater Road and wound up bathed in manure. An unidentified source in the county courthouse said a call came in suggesting something had been lost in the manure pond behind the milking barn. It is unknown what the lost item was, although sources suggested a baby doll was recovered near the pond. Director Simpson could not be reached before press time to confirm these details or to say if his search of the manure pond was successful. Sheriff Minor's office denied receiving a call or report of anything or anyone missing, although they did get an anonymous report suggesting there had been a prank call to the courthouse about the slop pond. After seeing the picture of the director in the manure pond and reviewing the facts, Sheriff Minor made this statement: "The Department of Homeland Security is overseen by the county commissioners' office. One can only guess why they would have their director wading around in a manure pit." The county commissioners were unavailable for comment.

Boog started Monday with his regular routine, sweeping the halls and emptying the trashcans before anyone else arrived in the courthouse. Then he made a large canister of coffee for the employee lounge before retiring to his office to wait for the mail. He heard Mabel exit the elevator exactly at eight-thirty-three and shuffle down the hall. Passing his office, she stopped, turned, looked at Boog with an ingratiating smile, and said, "Booger, Booger, Booger, what are we going to do with you? I hope you learned a lesson from this. You should know after being around this firetrap for as long as you have that nothing is what it seems. You can't trust anyone. Just remember that." She turned and walked into her office.

Boog scratched his head and wondered how she knew about the incident at the farm. Over the weekend, he had analyzed the spoof and considered all its implications. Obviously, Bud was the instigator, but the agonizing part was Stella's participation. She was the one that alerted him, which would have been normal, but he had requested she call the sheriff to confirm the report or have them dispatch help. Since none came, he had to assume she didn't follow his instruction, and the only reasonable explanation was that she knew about the plan. That part hurt. Stella had become a friend and he looked forward to their morning chat and her occasional visit to his trailer. They had even attended church together once, meeting in the morning and walking to the chapel.

The elevator opened, and he expected to hear Stella's familiar fast-paced gate to his door. Instead, he recognized the slow determined steps of Chet Sadinski. Sadinski walked past Boog's door, and without any hesitation in his step or turning his head said, "Boog, get your ass in my office."

Boog walked by Mabel, and she kept her head down, looking at a pile of papers on her desk, unflinching as if she were cast in stone. He proceeded into the commissioners' inner sanctum, finding Sadinski by himself, sitting at his desk, reading the *Hinkley Messenger*.

Boog stood next to the vacant chair in front of the desk and waited. Sadinski slowly looked up from the paper then turned it around so Boog could see the front page. He leaned down to get a closer look at the picture, reluctant realization hitting him square in the face as he recognized the mass of manure standing in the pond. He slowly rose to an erect stance and said, "Kind of got fooled by some of the boys around town. I was careful not to get the Hummer dirty. I put a towel on the seat."

Sadinski sat, still holding the paper in front of Boog, staring at him, motionless, and started quietly, slowly building to a crescendo. "I don't care about the seats. I don't care about boys playing tricks." Sadinski slowly rose from his chair as his voice grew louder. "What I care about is you making me look like a fool. A goddamn idiot for making you a department head. Do you remember what we talked about? Do you remember anything?" Sadinski ran his fingers through his hair, shaking his head in disgust and walked around his desk, throwing the paper in the trash. "I said—we all said—" He slowed his pronunciation to a sluggish pace. "Don't do anything unless we tell you to. Do you remember that?"

Boog opened his mouth to reply, but didn't have the chance.

"But no, you have to go swimming in Smith's shit pond, and not only that, call the newspaper, and have them take pictures." Sadinski got in front of Boog and placed his hands on his shoulders, staring straight into his eyes. "What the hell were you thinking? Wait. Let me rephrase that. Why didn't you think about what you were doing?"

Boog finally had an opportunity to reply. "There was a child—they said there was a child drowned in the pond. I couldn't just walk away. I'm sorry. There was a tiny shirt and a doll baby lying next to the pond. I couldn't just walk away."

"That's not what the paper says," Sadinski said sarcastically. "The paper doesn't say anything about a child. The paper, in so many words, says I'm an ass and you're a moron. That's all it says." Sadinski dropped his hands and paced around the office. "Minor is just loving this, too."

Mabel stuck her head into the office and said, "Stella is here and needs to see you."

"Can't you see I'm busy? Tell her to come back later—tomorrow or something."

"She says it's—well, it's about Boog, and this mess you all are discussin'."

"How do you know what we are discussing?" Sadinski said cocking his head, sensing an opportunity to entrap Mabel, his favorite prey.

"The way you are yelling, everyone at this end of town knows what you are talking about. You want to talk to her or not?" Mabel said, puffing out her cheeks in exasperation.

"Oh, what the hell. It can't get any worse." Sadinski slouched down in his chair and rested his head in his palm, waiting for Stella to come into the office.

Stella poked her head through the door as if checking for an all-clear and then slid in, standing with her hand still on the doorknob, maintaining an easy escape route.

Sadinski said, "What do you want to add to this mess? Don't tell me you're involved, too."

"Well," Stella said with hesitation. "Not exactly. But my ex-husband is, or was—or, anyway, it was him that did this. He made Smitty or one of his friends call about the kid drowning and knew Boog would come to help. He is just jealous because Boog is, you know, someone important. I should have known when they called, but they said they called the sheriff, too, so it sounded like it was real. And then when I called the sheriff's office—" Stella started to cry. "They said it was just a hoax, but Boog had already left, and I don't know, it's just all my fault. Don't you see? Boog just did what he thought was right." Stella came over to Boog and hugged him, still crying. "I'm sorry, Boog. I'm so sorry."

"Enough with the soap opera already," Sadinski said gruffly. "All right, we get the point. Anything else?"

Stella rubbed her nose on her sleeve. "I guess not. Just that it doesn't seem fair to blame Boog. What if there had been a baby in that pond? What then?"

"Instead of schmucks, we'd all be heroes, wouldn't we? Unfortunately, that didn't happen. I mean—well, you know what I mean. Anyway, we get your point." Sadinski raised his voice, looking toward the cracked office door. "Mabel, you get the point?"

Mabel didn't answer but they all heard her slam a drawer shut.

"Anything else you wish to add, Stella?"

"Well, I guess not. I mean, I think Boog should get an award or something for doing what he did. And I think someone should go arrest Bud O'Reilly for making a false report. There, I said it." She squeezed Boog's arm, turned, and left the room.

Sadinski still sat, contemplating what he had heard. "Well, I guess you meant well, and there is nothing the sheriff is going to do since he don't have a dog in this fight. We'll just have to weather the storm. But damn it, Boog, don't go off half-cocked again. Now go clean something or hide somewheres."

Boog turned and started for the door and Sadinski asked, "So, Boog, what was it like swimming in that manure pit?"

He stopped at the door. "Well, I guess it was as bad as you probably think. I had to throw all my clothes out."

"That what smelled so bad in the dumpster this morning? It's clear across the parking lot from my car, and I could still smell it."

"I'm just glad I didn't find anything in that pit. That would have been a lot worse than any smell," Boog said, leaving the office.

Chapter 16

The elevator door opened and the fast-paced click of heel hitting floor identified Stella before she slid to a halt, grabbing the door, her hair falling loosely around her shoulders. "Hey, Boog."

"Hey, Stell." Boog was just wasting time, waiting for the mail to arrive. "Where's the mail?"

"Wasn't any. What'cha doin'? Want to go to lunch? Ralphy's has half-priced burgers today. It's his five-year anniversary; burgers are half-price, and drinks are just a nickel. It's a steal. Wanna go?"

Boog smiled. He loved the girlish, almost childish lilt to her voice and manner. "I'll have to go get some money from the trailer, but yeah, I'd like to catch a burger."

"I'll buy. It's the least I can do after all that happened. Pick me up downstairs at noon." Before he could agree, she was off running back to the elevator.

They walked slowly down Main Street to Ralphy's, a converted storefront that boasted the coldest beer in town and the largest burgers. The noon lunch crowd had grown to near capacity due to the anniversary pricing, and they had to wait for someone to vacate a booth before ordering. Boog heard a few whispers referring to his slop pit episode and some laughing that went along with the shaking heads, but nothing that could ruin his lunch, which consisted of a cheeseburger, French fries smothered in chili and cheese, and a coke. Stella ordered a burger and shared his fries. They sat across from one another and leaned in, ignoring the noisy crowd, enjoying the abundance of food, talking and laughing in low tones, reminiscent of two kids in the high school cafeteria.

Boog faced the restaurant entrance and noticed, but did not make eye contact with, Bud O'Reilly when he entered and walked to the bar across the room. Bud slapped a few bar patrons on the back, saluted Ralphy behind the bar loud enough for all to hear and turned, leaning backwards with his elbows against the bar, and stared directly at Boog and Stella for a long, intense minute. Then he picked up his fresh beer and strolled over to their booth, stopping a few feet away, raising his head in the air, and sniffing, like a fox catching a scent. He smiled, looked around the room, went through the sniffing routine for those he felt had missed the first act and said, “I’m getting the faint odor of cow manure over here.” He looked down and picked up one of his feet, over-emphasizing the gesture. “Ain’t me.” Then he raised his nose again and leaned toward Boog and Stella. “Seems to be comin’ from over here.” This brought a few chuckles from the crowd, and Bud broke out in a boisterous laugh.

Boog said, “Hey, Bud.”

Stella stared at her burger without remark, but Boog saw the tears starting to form in her eyes, and without further consideration, decided he had had enough. He slowly pulled himself from the booth and stood up, saying softly, “Bud, you have a minute? I need to talk to you.” He hesitated for a second and then added with some emphasis, “Outside.”

Bud looked around the room, making sure he was the center of attention. “Well, now, what is it you want to see me about, Booger? You need me to hose you down, or maybe—”

Boog turned and walked toward the back of the restaurant and the rear door.

Bud yelled at Boog’s back. “Hey, where you goin’? I’m just trying to help here.”

The restaurant had grown quiet, with the exception of the clatter of dishes being washed and the occasional expletives of the cook preparing the many orders. Boog reached the rear door and turned. Bud was still standing next to the booth, holding his beer, watching.

Boog raised his voice, “This will just take a minute. Bud, step outside with me. I just need to clear something up.”

Bud looked around the room, suddenly not wanting to be the center of attention anymore, cleared his throat, took a swig of beer, and moved back to the bar, where he nuzzled in between two other patrons.

Boog still stood at the rear door and raised his voice again, saying slowly this time, "Bud, you comin'?"

Bud stared at the back bar, his hand wrapped around the beer glass. "Som bitch thinks I'm wastin' my time with him, he's nuts. Retard. He's nothin' but a damn retard."

As Boog started back toward the front of the restaurant in a direct line to the bar, Bud abruptly pushed his beer away, turned, and headed for the front door and exited without looking back.

Boog slowed his pace, turned, walked back to his booth, sat down, and picked up a French fry. "I just wanted to get some things straight; I didn't mean to scare him off like that. I don't think he even had his lunch," he said chomping on the French fry and picking up his burger for another bite. The boisterous atmosphere of the restaurant returned, and Boog smiled at Stella. "How's your burger?"

Stella stared at him, an uncomprehending look on her face. "What were you planning on doing in the alley? Just talk? Bud didn't think so. I've never seen him turn so white. Tell me—what were you going to do?"

"I was going to explain to him that he needed to quit making you upset. And if that took some persuasion other than talk, well, so be it." Boog took another bite and smiled while he chewed. "I told you before, Bud's a big talker. Too bad he drinks so much. He probably wouldn't get so worked up if he didn't drink. I think he's a nice guy down deep."

"You don't need to tell me about the drinking. I put up with it for too long," Stella said, starting to relax a little. "But aren't you a little afraid of him? I mean, he's a pretty big guy."

"Tug said fear can take on many forms; it's different for each person. Some people get sick from fear, afraid to go outside, afraid to step into the street, even afraid of themselves—what they might do if or when they lose control. Others show no fear, but carry a great burden from what their lack of fear allowed them to do, like in the war. Some people really fear pain. Am I afraid of Bud? Not really. If he had followed me, we would have talked, just like I said, but when we finished, he would have understood that it was time for him to stop bothering you." Boog moved the food tray around, trying to occupy his hands since all of the food was now gone. "Since he didn't follow me, I guess he figured it out on his own."

Stella sat back in the booth, sighed, and said, "Boog, I have never, ever been around anyone like you. You are the smartest person I have ever met."

"I might be the luckiest guy you ever met, but not the smartest," Boog said with his boyish smile. "I think it's time to go back to work. I might get fired again."

They both laughed and walked out of the restaurant, Stella searching for and finding his hand as they walked down Main Street toward the courthouse.

Sitting in his parked pickup truck, Bud watched them leave Ralphy's and steamed, feeling his blood pressure peek under his John Deere cap. "Freakin' retard som bitch," Bud said to himself. "Holdin' hands with my wife…" Bud growled, slamming his hands on the steering wheel.

An elderly man walking with a cane ambled by his open passenger window and looked in while Bud punished the steering wheel.

"What you lookin' at, you old geezer? Som bitch is stealin' my childrens' mother, and he ain't gonna get away with it." The old man took several steps back from the truck and hurried on his way.

Sheriff Minor came from the opposite direction, strolling toward Ralphy's for the bargain prices and to mingle with the potential voters. He heard Bud yelling at the old man and stepped up to the open window, leaned over, and looked in at Bud. "Got a problem, Bud? You look all, let's say, bothered about something. You ain't full of beer already this morning, are you? Damn, Bud, you need to get a grip here. I can't have you driving all over town drunk. We've talked about this before."

"I ain't drunk. I only had one beer before my whole day got ruin't. And hell, it's your fault—making that retard Booger some kind o' big shot. I'm in Ralphy's, thinkin' about havin' a cheap burger, and he comes up, gets right in my face, and tries to take me out back. Wants to kick my ass." He forced a chuckle. "Like he could or something. I kept my cool, tried not to make a scene or nothin'. Just told him to calm down, but he wouldn't have none of it. Finally, I had to leave or knock him out, which I knew was a bad idea, seein' how the whole place was packed to the gills. Sheriff, you got to do something about that boy, he's outta hand."

Minor stood up, adjusted his Stetson, and brushed his shirt-sleeves free of wrinkles while he considered what he had just heard. "This got anything to do with Stella?" Minor asked, not facing Bud, smiling and waving at a couple passing on the other side of the street.

"What? Come on, Sheriff, we been divorced for goin' on three years. Maybe he's havin' trouble fillin' my shoes, if you know what I mean, but as long as he stays away from my kids… I mean, you never know what that retard might do around kids."

Minor looked back into the window and stared at Bud. "Maybe he was just pissed about the slop pit thing you pulled."

Bud fell silent for a minute, trying to decide the legal implications of an admission of guilt. "Uh, I don't know nothin' about that. I mean—"

"Sure, Bud. I already talked to Smitty. Okay, you put one over on Boog. Everybody had a good laugh, but I'd say he has a pretty good reason to be upset, wouldn't you?"

Bud gave the question some thought and said in a solemn reply, "Don't give him no right."

"Bud, go home and forget about it. I've never seen Boog raise his voice about anything. Never seen him hit anybody, either. I don't think you have anything to worry about. And the thing about your kids—that's bullshit, too, and you know it. So the way I see it, you pulled a fast one on Boog. Maybe he did get in your face about it. Probably had a right to, and it's all over. Am I right? It's all over?" Minor said sternly.

Bud stared straight ahead, at first not replying, and then said, "Whatever."

"Good. Damn, now there's a line out the door at Ralphy's. Maybe I need to inspect the kitchen today. See you later, Bud." Sheriff Minor touched the brim of his hat in salutation and resumed his stroll toward Ralphy's, waving at the occasional passing car.

Chapter 17

The elevator door opened, and Stella skidded to a stop at Boog's office door. "Hey, Boog."

"Hey, Stell. Any mail?"

"A whole bunch of stuff and right here on top is something official from Washington. Look, it's got an official seal on the back and the envelope feels real expensive." Stella's eyes were beaming and her grin was never ending, as if it was painted on her face. "Open it," she demanded.

As usual, Boog inspected the envelope, front and back, held it up to the light, sniffed it, and gave it back to Stella. "Here, you open it." He knew she was bursting with curiosity about the contents.

Stella ripped open the envelope as if it were a long-anticipated Christmas gift and pulled out an invitation. She opened the folded card and read. "You are cordially invited to the annual awards banquet of the Federal Department of Homeland Security on the third of November, held in the Grand Banquet Hall of the Washington Hyatt Regency on Capital Hill. RSVP. Attire: formal, black tie optional." Stella slowly raised her head and stared at Boog. "Jeez, the Hyatt Regency in Washington. How you gonna get there?"

"What? Me? I'm not going to Washington. Come on, Stella, that's for some kind of, you know, public official—like one of the commissioners or something. Just give it to Mabel, and she'll give it to Mister Sadinski." Boog started looking through the numerous catalogues and credit card solicitations. "Look at this; they'll give me up to thirty thousand dollars for any way I want to use it. They don't even know who I am."

"Boog," Stella said sternly. "This isn't addressed to Sadinski. It's addressed to you. It says right here, Jasper Simpson, Department of Homeland Security, Hinkley County. It doesn't get any plainer than that."

Boog reached into his desk drawer. "I wonder if that has anything to do with this." He held another unopened manila envelope addressed the same as the invitation. "This came in Saturday's mail. I forgot about it. I was saving it for you to open, since you know more about this stuff than I do. It's probably just another one of those special warnings like all of the others. Switch to orange alert, or green or blue or something."

Stella grabbed the envelope. "Jeez, Boog, don't stick stuff like that in that stupid drawer. It could be important." Stella opened the envelope and read, skipping over unimportant sentences. "Let's see, the annual meeting of the Department of Homeland Security is being held in Washington. Jeez, Boog; it's the day before the awards banquet. It says you have to attend. It says every department head is required to attend. States with letters beginning with A to J will be staying at the Hyatt. You already have a room for two days; your travel has already been arranged. Look, there's an itinerary stapled to the letter. You fly out of O'Hare. Wow, it's first-class on United. You get there on Wednesday night, and come back on Friday. It even says they will have a limo waiting for you when you get to Dulles." Stella was doing her excited tap dance while she read. "Dulles must be the airport in Washington. It says you are to use your DHS credit card for all other expenses. What credit card?" Stella turned the envelope upside down but nothing fell out.

"Oh," Boog said, casually opening his desk drawer. "This came with all the other stuff when they delivered the Hummer and trailer. He tossed a credit card down on the desk.

Stella picked it up and inspected it. "An American Express card. It just says Federal DHS." She turned it over and read, "The bearer of this card must show federal identification before use." She looked up at Boog. "Have you used this?"

"Are you kidding? I've never used a credit card in my life. Why would I need a credit card? I don't know anything about those things," he said, as if touching it could spread a rash.

Stella said, "Stay here." She turned and walked out toward the commissioners' office. Entering Mabel's office, she laid the letter and itinerary down in front of her. "Something you might want to bring to Mister Sadinski's attention." Stella said with a cynical tone. "I suspect he's not going to be too happy, seein' how he didn't get an invitation. You might want to put it on your calendar that Boog'll be gone for a few days."

Mabel looked over the letter and itinerary, looked up with her deeply inset black eyes, and glared at Stella, but then a stiff smile cracked the surface, joining Stella's seemingly static grin. "You're right; this is gonna hurt him like a boil on his hind quarters. I suspect you better take Boog shopping. He's gonna need some traveling clothes; that is, if'n he doesn't get fired again." They both laughed.

• • •

Stella prepared Boog for his adventure by outfitting him in a new sport coat, shirt, tie, and matching pants. There were new slip-on shoes with tassels that he suggested were girlish. He threatened to cut them off, but relented when Stella protested. She packed all of his other necessities in a suitcase she provided and they prepared for the three-hour drive to the airport. Stella insisted on chauffeuring him in her car, especially after Sadinski blew a proverbial gasket and refused to allow use of the Hummer. Since the letter had mandated the director's appearance and quashed the commissioners' plans for a paid vacation to Washington, their only available retribution was to refuse to allow use of the Hummer for transportation to the airport. They were unaware of the federal credit card and assumed the financial demands of the trip would cause Boog to relinquish his position, allowing Sadinski to make the trip in his absence. When it became apparent that their plan was failing, the commissioners called an emergency meeting, grilling Boog on his finances and ability to represent the county at such an important meeting. In the end, Bellows and Featherstone blamed Sadinski for his poor judgment in hiring Boog and resolved to take action at the next commissioners' meeting, which meant they would take no action.

As the hour for departure grew near, Boog stewed over the thought of airplanes, hotels, meetings, and banquets, and with each passing minute, it caused greater distress. As he waited for Stella to pull in front of the trailer to pick him up for their trip to Chicago, he decided life as a director was not so great after all. He would forget the trip, march into the commissioners' office, and quit. If no one was there, he would just hand the Hummer keys to Mabel and head for the boiler room. He was sure he could get his room back at the hardware store.

Stella wheeled her car in front of the trailer and honked. He felt the sweat gathering under his new dress shirt. She would be very disappointed, and that was a problem, because the last thing he wanted to do was disappoint Stella.

He opened the door to the trailer just wide enough to see her sitting in the car, leaning forward and looking up at him through the windshield. She waved her arm, indicating he needed to hurry. Okay, he thought, before I go to the commissioners' office, I will explain this to Stella. Try to make her understand. He stepped out of the trailer, suitcase in hand, opened the car door, and said meekly, "Hey, Stell."

"Let's go. We're late." She reached over, grabbed the suitcase, and flung it into the back seat. Then she grabbed Boog's arm, pulled him onto the seat, and put the car in gear. Boog slammed the door shut to avoid falling out.

"Stell, there's something we need to talk about."

Stella wheeled out of the parking lot and tromped on the gas flying down Main Street. "It's a three-hour drive, and we need to make up some time. I had to get gas and drop the kids off, and I wanted to get you some snacks. I heard they don't give you anything on airplanes anymore. I mean, they used to treat everyone to lunch and stuff, but now it's just peanuts. So I got you a sandwich and some chips, a couple of candy bars, and some gum. I also heard that if they go up too fast, and you don't chew gum, your ears will pop, and then you'll have to wear hearing aids for the rest of your life. You ever hear that? You excited? Boy, I would be if I was goin' to Washington, staying in a big hotel, and meeting all those important people."

They were already out of town and headed for the four-lane. It was too late to explain that he wasn't going to Washington, so Boog just slumped down in his seat and pondered the imponderable.

• • •

O'Hare International was an unending maze of one hundred and eighty-degree turns and large signs announcing the disorderly transition from ground dweller to air passenger. Boog was totally lost in the confusing mishmash of arrows, letters, and colors directing the flow of arriving and departing passengers. After several errant turns, Stella finally found a short-term parking lot and with passive directives ordered Boog to hurry this way and that way until they arrived at the United ticket counter. The line wrapped around itself five times, and time was slipping away, with departure scheduled in less than an hour.

Stella finally grabbed Boog's arm and pulled him out of the line to a vacant station where an attendant was diligently working on a computer. Stella announced their presence by clearing her throat. "Ahem. Excuse me."

The young man looked up briefly and then returned to his work. "Go to the end of the line. And before you say it, everyone's plane is leaving shortly. Be patient."

Stella looked at Boog and then sternly back at the attendant. "Mister Simpson, show this—" she hesitated and then emphasized, "gentleman your identification."

Boog started to protest and then wondered, what identification?

Stella whispered, "Show him your wallet, Boog; you know, the one from Washington."

Boog said, "Oh," and flipped the bi-fold wallet open to reveal his deputy federal marshal badge. He was about to say that he was just a guy from Hinkley County and that circumstances he didn't understand provided the badge, but it was too late.

"Oh, my," was all the attendant said, jumping over the counter. "Come this way, Mister Simpson."

They walked down the busy terminal to a special door that required a keyed password to enter. The door opened, and inside was a room with plush chairs and several writing stands, a private bar with attendant, and several well-dressed men either working quietly on laptop computers or conversing softly over drinks. After entering, the attendant said, "Your itinerary, please, Mister Simpson."

Stella handed the attendant the itinerary and said, "Look, Mister Simpson doesn't usually do this type of thing, I mean, fly all around the country. He will need some help—some direction, if you know what I mean. Can you do that?" Stella pulled at her purse and opened it, searching for something. She eventually pulled out a five-dollar bill and held it out for the attendant with a look of satisfaction. "Maybe this will help."

The attendant looked at the five-dollar bill and then up at Stella and Boog. "Ah, no need for that, madam. I am sure one of the personal assistants will be happy to help Mister Simpson."

Stella looked around the room. "What personal assistant?" There was a tone in Stella's voice that implied the title personal assistant sounded just a little too close and personal for her.

"I will have someone come directly." The attendant turned toward the door, rolling his eyes at the bartender, and exited.

"Okay, Mister Jasper Simpson, deputy marshal and director of whatever, I want you to go to Washington and show 'em what it means to be one of Hinkley High's most honored. And another thing; well, it's something I have been meaning to tell you, but I—well, I mean—I love you, Boog, and I'm going to miss you while you're gone. I'm gonna pray for you, and well, I love you, okay? I can't help it." She put her arms around Boog and hugged him then kissed him long and hard and said very softly. "I do love you."

Stella turned and started for the door. It opened just as she reached for the handle. A smartly dressed young lady with a badge around her neck entered and walked right up to Boog. "Mister Simpson?" Her blonde hair was cut short, and her tailored skirt fit tightly and was cut just above the knee. She wore medium heels and a sweater vest over a button-down shirt that said "strictly business." "If you will come with me, Mister Simpson, I will take you to your gate and get you seated and comfortable. Do you have a firearm? If you do, we will need to check that before you enter the secure area."

Stella stood at the door, looking at the posterior of the personal assistant, making a quick comparison, looking down at her loose fitting pants, flat-heeled Hushpuppy loafers, and three-year-old blouse, and then made eye contact with Boog. He had not moved an inch since Stella made her proclamation, and he saw the irritation in her expression. She bent her lips into a smile, blew him a kiss, and walked out through the open door.

Boog was led through a private hallway that exited into the security checkpoint. He was again led to the front of the line, where he showed his identification and was passed without scrutiny. A golf cart was waiting, and they were whisked off to his gate. The assistant did not engage him in conversation or even ask his destination. Arriving at the gate, he was taken down the ramp with no questions asked and promptly seated in the first row of first-class. The assistant said, "Mister Simpson, I hope you have a pleasant flight and thank you for choosing United." She exited the aircraft.

Boog turned and looked around. He was the only one on the plane, at least as far as he could see. A flight attendant appeared from behind a wall and said, "Good morning, Mister Simpson. The rest of the passengers will be boarding in a few minutes. Can I get you anything? Juice, coffee, perhaps a cocktail?"

The turmoil and tension of this whole affair churned in his stomach, and he knew it would not be wise to add to the brew. "No, thank you."

The attendant disappeared. The discomfort in his stomach grew worse the longer he sat, and he knew there was no way he could avoid a trip to the men's room before departure. Boog stood and walked toward the exit, meeting the attendant near the forward galley.

"Can I help you? Coffee, tea, juice?"

"Do I have time to find a bathroom?" Boog asked. No reason to be shy at this point. If he didn't find a bathroom soon, there would be no reason to ask.

"There's a facility right here." She stepped next to Boog and opened a bi-fold door. Boog now heard other passengers approaching the door through the jet way. He looked through the opening at the compartment, which was even smaller than the bathroom in his travel trailer. He looked at the attendant and then back at the compartment. She was waiting for him to move so she could welcome the other passengers.

Boog squeezed himself into the compartment and closed the door, throwing the latch. His head touched the ceiling, which followed the contour of the airplane fuselage, as he looked down at the little toilet built into the corner of the room. He was not a big man by any means, but fitting himself into the space provided and conducting a major elimination of nastiness—well, it just didn't seem possible. Momentary anxiety made him want to open the door and run, get out of this confined space, out of the airport, back to the secure confines of the courthouse boiler room, but he could wait no longer, so he prepared for the inevitable and maneuvered into position, accidentally hitting the flush button with his elbow. The whoosh of the pressure vacuum mechanism along with the bong, bong, bong of the warning bell advising him that departure was fast approaching and the compartment must be vacated, caused him to jump up, hitting his head on the ceiling, bringing a twinkle of stars as he sat back on the seat.

Exiting the compartment, walking back to his seat, and rubbing his head, he felt his composure return and decided his fate was cast. There was no way to stop the progression of events, so he made up his mind to relax and try to endure the adventure ahead.

The plane ride was actually an enjoyable diversion from his anxiety. He took Stella's advice and diligently chewed gum throughout the flight, satisfied that he had avoided any damage to his hearing. He was one of the first passengers exiting the jet way into the terminal at Dulles, and a man dressed in black with a chauffeur hat held a placard with "Simpson" scribbled in red. Boog approached him hesitantly, realizing Simpson was a relatively common name.

The man consulted a clipboard in his hand and said slowly, reading, "Are you Jasper Simpson? From Hinkley?"

Boog smiled, appreciating the recognition in this strange new place. "Yes, sir, that's me." Boog leaned over and consulted the clipboard as well. "Right there, that's my name."

"I presume you have some luggage, Mister Simpson?" the man asked.

"Call me Boog, okay? I've got a suitcase, so's I suppose we need to wait a few minutes until they bring it off the plane."

The driver stared at Boog in disbelief, then caught himself and explained, "The baggage claim is downstairs, so we have a little walk. You are the only pick-up this trip, so we can go now. It's this way."

Boog looked at his nametag and said, "Fine by me, Roger. That plane was getting a little cramped. And that toilet, have you ever used one of them things?" He rubbed his head again. "'Bout knocked myself out."

Roger just shook his head, thinking, *And I thought I had seen it all.* "So this is your first trip to Washington I take it?"

"First trip anywhere," Boog said, walking and gawking at the horde of passengers, vendors, and airline personnel hustling in every direction. "Why are they all in such a hurry? They can't all be late."

"There's no such thing as 'on time' in this town. Everyone is late. If you're on time, it means you aren't very busy and must not be important. If you're too late, it means you don't care enough and should not be appreciated. So you have to be just late enough to raise an eyebrow, but not late enough to piss anyone off. It's called being fashionably late. Your first lesson on how to be politically correct in Washington, Goober."

"It's Boog."

"Oh, yeah. Sorry, I get so many passengers; it's tough to keep the names straight. Especially the more common names."

They arrived at the baggage claim just as the bags were being distributed. They waited as the bags passed. Gucci, Armani, fake Gucci, fake Armani, and then a suitcase that looked like something you would find in your grandmother's attic—fake brownish-orange woven straw with leather binding and a fake plastic bone handle.

"That's mine," Boog said, reaching for the bag.

"Never would have guessed," Roger said sarcastically leading them through the automatic doors. The stretch limo was parked one lane over, surrounded by no parking signs, its emergency lights flashing and motor running. A large sign was conspicuously posted in the windshield—DHS Pickup—Special Security Clearance. A policeman was standing nearby, and Roger tipped his hat as they walked by. "You're at the Hyatt Capital, right?"

Boog reached into his shirt pocket and pulled out a little slip of paper that Stella had prepared for him with the name of the hotel, name of the airport, name of the city, and finally, her telephone number both at home and at the courthouse. She had also given him a quick lesson how to operate the DHS cell phone that he had revealed to her about the same time he made the credit card known. "That's it. Hyatt Hotel. Is it far?"

"Half-hour on a good traffic day. Today, an hour. Sit back, turn the TV on, make some calls, have a drink; you're in the big city now, Goober." The smoked glass partition separating the driver from the passenger compartment went up, and Roger disappeared. Boog looked around the plush interior of the limo.

There was enough room for eight, maybe ten people. There was a refrigerator, a small glass-front case with glasses and other utensils, a master control panel for all sorts of electronics, a TV and DVD hanging overhead, and a large, smoked-glass window in the roof. He pulled out the cell phone and flipped the thin device open. Inside the flip phone was a small paper on which Stella had printed instructions for use of the phone. He took out his other instruction sheet and punched in Stella's home phone since she had taken the balance of the day off. The phone rang only once.

"Hi, Boog. Are you there yet? I could tell it was you by the caller ID. I never got a call before that said 'federal government.' Where are you?"

Boog was holding the phone to his ear, but since the phone did not seem big enough to reach his mouth, he put the phone in front of his face and yelled when he spoke. "I'm in the limo, and Roger is taking me to the hotel." Then he put the phone back to his ear, hoping Stella would respond. He caught her in the middle of a reply.

"—don't have to yell. I told you; just hold the phone to your ear. Anyway, who's Roger?"

He held the phone out and yelled, "Roger's the limo guy that holds the sign in the airport. He's pretty smart. Knows where to get your luggage and all about the airport. He just can't remember names very well. Keeps callin' me Goober." He brought the phone back to his ear.

"—me again when you get to the hotel. I want to hear all about it. I love you, and tell Roger your name's not Goober. Call me later."

Boog held the phone in front of his face. "Okay." When he put it back to his ear, there was another voice.

"—you wish to re-place this call, hit seven. If you wish to place another call, hit six. If you wish—"

He held the phone out again. "No, thanks," and closed the flip side of the phone. He wondered what Roger was doing so he went to the window and knocked, and the window slid down, revealing Roger and the front seat of the limo. "Hey, Roger."

"Hey, Goob."

"It's Boog. How long?"

"You need to stop or something? I can get off the freeway if you gotta use the head or something," Roger said, keeping his eye on the traffic.

"No, just wondering. It's kind of quiet back here. So, you live in Washington? I guess that's kind of a dumb question. You must live here since you work here," Boog said, answering his own question.

"Actually, I don't live here. I live more north, toward Baltimore. The livery service garage is on the north side, outside of D.C. and I pick a car up everyday and drive in. I live out toward Roxbury. I used to live in the city, but you had to count the hours every night and pray you didn't get shot before the sun came up, and then it wasn't a sure bet you'd make it to work. I was lucky and found a dumpy house in a small neighborhood before the prices went out of sight. It didn't hurt having an old lady that's a nurse, so the two of us can make it—barely. You from Chicago?"

Boog laughed. "Hardly. That was the first time I ever been to Chicago, when I went to the airport. I'm from Hinkley County. That's about three hours from Chicago. I'm the director of homeland security for the county. They made me come here for a meeting; otherwise, I wouldn't be doin' this."

"Yeah, I've picked up a whole bunch of goobers from all over. Let me give you some pointers, just as I told all the others. This ain't like down on the farm. Everyone you meet, talk to, or bump into is looking to get in your pocket, and that includes the politicians. Someone asks you a question—keep walking. Someone asks you what time it is, tell 'em you don't know or don't answer. Keep your money in your sock or zipped up with your privates, although that probably ain't safe here, either, or someplace a hand can't reach it. Don't leave anything valuable in your room because it won't be there when you get back. Don't walk anywhere where you might be alone, even for a second, because you'll end up with a knife in your back and no Timex. Even if it's a so-called public building or some kind of special political place, stay alert. Hell, we've had 'em killed in the restroom of the Congressional Office Building. The only thing that got the guy was a free airplane ride home. You go out at night, take a taxi from the door of the hotel to the door of the place you're goin'. Don't let the hack drop you a block away 'cause he got another fare. And finally, if you pick up a hooker, don't give her any money until you done. And then, no matter how good she was, don't show her no more money than what she was askin'. Don't go to any room she recommends. If you do, you won't come out; at least, not with any money or clothes; you're lucky to come out at all. Don't tell her to come see you and give her your pass number or pass key. If you do, you might as well slip all your money under the door for anyone walking by to take it. You want her to come to your room, meet her in the lobby or give the bell captain a twenty and have him escort her to your room. That way, she knows someone can identify her if she rousts you or has someone else with her. You got all that, Goob? Other than those tips, you should have a good time, 'specially since it's all free. Some of these guys I picked up said they had the key to the treasury—that's the government American Express card. That's a gold mine, man. They give you one?" Boog hesitated for a second. "Smart, boy; you learn quick. Don't answer any questions about money, or anything else for that matter. None of my business, goober. See, there's gonna be a lot of people askin' you questions like that. You think, 'Oh he's a nice guy; won't hurt to answer his questions, tell him my business.' Next thing you know, you layin' in some alley, and he's out livin' the high life on yo' credit card."

Boog sat, staring through the open partition and the windshield at the seemingly infinite stream of cars and trucks stretching up the highway, absorbing all of the warnings and concluding that once he reached his destination, he would not leave until Roger picked him up for his return ride to the airport. "Will you be taking me back to the airport?"

"Not unless you call and ask for me. I'll give you a card, and you can call the dispatcher and make the request. Sometimes they'll do it if the money's right. Look, Goob, I'll be straight with you. I live off the tips. So far, runnin' you farmers from the airport is about to make me start beggin' on the street corner. Hell, this is the shortest week I've had in a long time. If I do get a tip, it's like two bits or something, and the rube wants me to heft his damn bags into the hotel."

Roger wheeled the limo past the cabstand and under the portico into the bright lights of the hotel. The bell captain opened the limo door, looked in, and welcomed Boog to the Hyatt before he blew a whistle and hustled away. Another attendant hustled to help Roger with the suitcase and both stood at the door as he exited the limo. There was a lingering silence before Roger shook his head and turned to walk around the rear of the limo. It took Boog a minute to put all of the pieces together—Stella's instructions that everyone will have their hands out wanting money, Roger's admission that lack of tips would be his ruination, and the lengthy pause and hesitation before walking away by each person that had helped him since he first arrived at the airport.

"Hey, Roger," Boog yelled, reaching him just as he started to close the driver's door of the limo. "Wait a minute." Boog looked around, feeling self-conscious about what he had to do, but then thought, hey, it was Roger's advice that made him do it. Boog took his shoe off, pulled his pant leg up a little, and took off his sock. He fished out some folded bills and handed Roger a ten. "Thanks for all your advice and help at the airport."

Roger held the ten with two fingers at arm's length from his face and daintily laid it on the front seat of the limo. "My pleasure, Goob. You have a good time and remember what I told you." Boog was still standing next to the car with his bare foot, and Roger pointed at it. "Better get that covered up and find someplace else to keep your money. I don't think it's a secret anymore." He pulled the door shut and pulled away, leaving Boog with his exposed bare foot in the middle of the unloading zone with the bellhop and a line of patrons waiting for other transportation staring at him.

His spacious room was on the tenth floor. The walkway in front of the door was open to the atrium overlooking the hotel lobby, restaurant, and fountain. It was nicely decorated with a wet bar and well-stocked refrigerator. Boog dropped another five dollars in the hand of the bellhop as he exited the room and realized that, at this rate, the eighty dollars he had brought would be exhausted before the end of the day. There was a fresh bouquet of flowers and a bottle of wine with a note prominently displayed next to an overstuffed chair. He had not experienced such luxury before and stood spellbound, surveying the many accoutrements of the room. He eventually inspected the note attached to the wine bottle: "Jasper, welcome to Washington. The folder on the desk contains your itinerary for tomorrow. I hope we have a chance to get together while you are here. Marty."

The itinerary gave him locations and a schedule of meetings and events for the attendee, and each meeting was highlighted by a speaker of political notoriety or one of the politically appointed leaders of the department. Each event was timed to coincide with breakfast, lunch, or the cocktail hour with the final awards banquet involving dinner.

Boog settled in for an evening of soft drinks and snacks from the stocked bar. He anticipated trying the canned pate' and packaged smoked sausage prominently displayed on top of the refrigerator. There was a knock on the door, cordial and not demanding. Boog, thinking that the bellhop had probably returned with friends for another handout, cautiously opened the door and found Marty, standing sentry with her back to the door, enjoying the view of the massive atrium and activities in progress below. She turned and smiled, her hair parted in the middle and seductively flowing over one eye, the other side twisted behind an ear. She wore a tailored lapelled jacket with the collar turned up and a silk scarf draped over her shoulders. Her blouse was opened, revealing a thin neckline and fine gold chain with a diamond pendant. She held a wine glass, nearly empty against her chest, and said, “Can I have a refill?”

“Hey, Marty.” He stepped back, allowing her to enter the room.

“I thought maybe I would see you downstairs in the lounge. It’s quite a spectacle down there—all kinds of people from all over the country.” She held out her glass, obviously expecting service. Boog took the glass, hesitated, and then remembered the wine bottle. Feeling less insecure now, realizing what she wanted—for the moment, anyway—he picked up the wine bottle and examined the top. There was a foil wrapper that he tediously removed using his pocketknife, only to reveal a cork stuck in the end. He poked at it with his knife without much success and finally looked up at Marty, who said, “I think you need a corkscrew. Let me give it a try.” She took the bottle and went to the wet bar, retrieving a corkscrew.

Boog’s cell phone chirped, pleading for him to answer. He picked up the phone, studied it, and hit the talk button, bringing it to his ear.

“Hey, Boog,” Stella said. “How’s it goin’? Everything okay? You find the hotel?”

“Hey, Stell,” Boog said holding the phone out. “Uh, everything is okay. The hotel is very, uh, fancy. Real big.”

Marty pulled the cork from the bottle, reached for a clean glass, and said, “Jasper, you want some chardonnay? It’s very good.” She held the bottle out, inspecting the label. “Two thousand four, Nappa Valley.”

The cell phone erupted. “Who’s that? Is someone there? Where are you? Is there someone in your room?”

He held the phone out in front of his face and lingered, looking up at Marty with a look of puzzlement and finally said, "Uh, it's just Marty."

"Marty who? Marty the girl you told me about, the one that came when they brought the Hummer? That Marty, in your room? Alone?" Stella went silent, waiting for a reply.

Marty, sensing the personal nature of the call, sat the wine glass and bottle down, placed her finger to her mouth giving the international signal for silence, turned, and left the room. He raised the phone and said, "I didn't hear that last part, Stell; the TV was a little loud. Marty was here, uh, delivering some papers for tomorrow."

"Oh, and just happened to be there when I called. Well, you just have a great time in Washington, Mister Big Shot. And tell Marrrrty," she said in a snide drawl, "I said hi." The phone beeped, apparently indicating an end to the call.

•••

The following day's events went as scheduled—including a rousing welcoming ceremony accompanied by a buffet breakfast the likes of which Boog had never experienced. He tried to follow the lead of others in line as they filled their plates with glazed fruit tarts, smoked salmon accompanied by dollops of caviar on the side, eggs Benedict, and an abundant assortment of pastries and other sweet confections. The noon meeting involved a video presentation highlighting the many weather-related tragedies in which the Emergency Management Agency had involvement, featuring local politicians and EMA dignitaries with their sleeves rolled up surveying the debris from large helicopters and giving patronizing sound bites. Another segment highlighted the many terrorist plots the Department of Homeland Security had preempted by their pervasive community presence, ending with an impromptu sound bite by the president emphasizing his commitment to continued zealous funding of the department and his eternal thanks to the local department heads for their vigilant efforts in rooting out evil plots against our government. The presentation was followed by a table-served luncheon of unrecognizable gourmet selections, each consisting of one or two bites that seemed to please those sharing his table, but left Boog wondering when something of substance would be served.

The afternoon gave him a choice of a tour of the Capital Building or the Pentagon. Boog chose the Capital tour since Marty had sent him a note during the lunch suggesting she would be leading the tour. A shuttle bus was waved through security, and Boog's group was marched into the Capital rotunda to begin the tour. Marty gave a short introduction after nudging him to the front of the group and positioning him next to her. She looped her arm through his and led the group through the maze of hallways and rooms, describing as they walked the historic significance of the building and its artistic treasures. He was thoroughly amazed at her knowledge and composure as she casually regurgitated anecdotal historical highlights of each statue, mural, and tapestry while continually making personal contact, either by looping her arm through his or guiding him with an outstretched hand. The other members of the group tagged behind, occasionally interjecting a question, but mostly reveling in the grandeur of the premises and hiding their displeasure at her lack of personal attention for everyone except Boog.

The tour ended on the balcony of the Senate chambers as a lone senator decried the outrageous spending practices of the majority incumbent party with only a spattering of unofficial personnel lounging in the large hall, ignoring the rambling speech. Once the group was settled into their seats and given a short lesson on the convenience of closed circuit TV and C-Span, Marty led Boog out of the balcony into the adjoining hall.

"Did you enjoy the tour, learn how our government works?" Marty smiled, leaning against him with her arm still looped through his.

"That guy must be a terrible speaker. There was hardly anyone there to listen to what he said. Maybe he was just practicing. They probably all come in later, and he does it again." Boog felt satisfied in his assumption, going on to another question. "Everything seems to be in miniature. The halls seem so small and the stairways are so little. Why is that?"

"Well, when this place was built, two hundred years ago now, everyone was smaller for one, not big and muscular like you." She emphasized her complement by gently rubbing his bicep. "And architecture was limited to confined areas to conserve heat. Everything was heated by convection, with small stoves or fireplaces in each room; the smaller the room, the easier to maintain a tolerable temperature. Also, the building was designed to function as a place of government rather than a tourist attraction, so other than the rotunda and the adjoining chambers, smaller meeting rooms were most efficient."

Marty turned to face Boog, running her hands up his chest and straightening his shirt collar, smiling, enjoying the intimate contact. "Can you imagine? Think of the men that have stood right here, where we stand right now, discussing the latest legislation, the threats from abroad, deciding which pub at which they will later meet to secretly plan political strategy. Can we meet later to plan some political strategy?" The question was lost, intermingled with the historical perspective, and asked so nonchalantly. He did not answer as Marty continued to softly manipulate his shirt and rub the outline of his chest, her breath and pleasant scent drifting between them.

The intimacy was abruptly interrupted by a bald, plump, blue jean-attired member of their group who exited the chamber into the hall and said, "I have to pee; where's the head?" Looking at his Timex he added, "The awards banquet starts in an hour. When we leaving?"

Marty looked up at Boog, blew him a kiss with her smiling rouge lips, and turned to the impatient tourist. "The men's room is at the end of the hall. By the time you get through peeing, as you so eloquently put it, we will be ready to depart."

•••

The grand ballroom swelled with motion and activity as the many delegates from across the country converged for the banquet and ceremony. Boog handed his invitation to a tuxedo-clad doorman, who after examining the embossed name and invitation number, escorted him to one of the front tables, close to the podium. His new sport coat and trousers fit awkwardly; the coat was a little small across the chest and the striped tie choked him when he bent over to sit. The salesman at the JC Penney store had tied the tie and advised him to just loop it over his head and tighten with the small end. He did not give specific instruction on how tight, or on how to loosen it so blood could reach the brain.

The V.I.P. table loomed above the main floor with the podium at center stage. Nameplates adorned each position adjacent to the podium with Marty seated at the end. She was busy reviewing documents and talking with other important looking attendants who scurried here and there, whispering further instructions to still another layer of attendants apparently not important enough to approach the center stage. Several ominous looking men with wired earpieces, who Boog assumed were security guards, roamed the room, occasionally looking under tables or glancing toward the ceiling and rear balcony.

The meeting eventually came to order with opening remarks and an invocation by a navy chaplain. The five-course dinner took an hour to serve and included delicacies beyond Boog's imagination. He watched and attempted to mimic diners that appeared to know what they were eating and how to accomplish the act with finesse.

Following dinner, the acting secretary of homeland security was introduced and proceeded to give a detailed résumé of the accomplishments of the department since replacing the past acting secretary, who departed amidst scandalous rumors of rampant waste, corruption, and ineptitude. The current acting secretary assured the assembled group that he would soon be appointed permanent secretary and that the current scandalous rumors of rampant waste, corruption, and ineptitude were just that—scandalous rumors. The crowd offered boisterous shouts of praise and lengthy applause with each example of increased budget appropriations to further the cause of rooting out the evil that lurked in rural and suburban neighborhoods. Cheers rose from the floor with every example of unlimited distribution of cash to any that requested assistance from FEMA in declared natural disasters. A standing ovation lasting over five minutes was given when the acting secretary announced that each county department head would receive a cash advance of one thousand dollars on their federal American Express card to be used for special purchases in the event of an undeclared natural disaster that created a need to charge emergency expenses. Further shouts of praise rose when he added that it would not be necessary to formally account for these incidental expenses. At the same time that this announcement was being raucously praised, a pack of attendants moved through the room like spawning salmon, slipping political pledge cards with return envelopes next to each coffee cup, each plainly identifying that donations of up to one thousand dollars could legally be contributed by individuals and that charge cards were accepted.

The acting secretary concluded by raising his hands and quieting the crowd. The house lights were dimmed, and with a serious, almost tear-inspiring tone, he proceeded at great length and with idol inspired enthusiasm to introduce the guest of honor. Finally, as the crowd began to show its displeasure by yawning and adjusting their chairs he said, "Ladies and gentlemen, the president of the United States."

The president bounded onto the stage as the crowd erupted, cheering the grand entrance. The applause consumed the room for several minutes as the narrow spotlight framed the president. He shook hands with the acting secretary and raised their joined hands in a show of solidarity and friendship. As the applause faded and the crowd again took their seats, the president began his brief comments with praise of his personal friend, the acting secretary, his staff, and of course all of those in attendance. He reminded everyone of the continuing terrorist threat, his diligent fight against those who wished to undermine democracy and raise taxes, and his basic belief in the silent moral majority.

He then turned to the acting secretary and said, "Before I leave, I understand we have a special award tonight, is that right?"

The acting secretary stepped up, holding a large plaque with unrecognizable inscriptions. "Mister President, tonight we honor one of our own—a young man who sets an example for all of us. Someone like you, Mister President—a young man who places the safety of his community above his own, whose constant vigilance and responsive action at a local school brought prompt resolution to a very dangerous situation. Mister President, if you would be so kind to read the proclamation inscribed on this award and present it to our honoree."

"Why, it would be my pleasure. Let's see, uh, yes, here we go. 'For meri-tor-ious—'" He paused. "Man, that's a mouthful." The audience chuckled along with the president. "Let's see—'meritorious action in the face of danger and for outstanding leadership as a county department head of homeland security, now therefore, I—that's me, I guess—the president of the United States, do hereby recognize and commend Jasper Simpson and present this award."

There was a brief pause as the president hesitated, holding the award, looking at the acting secretary, who stared blankly back. "Well, uh, this is a darn nice award. Do we have someone to give it to?"

"Oh, my, yes. Uh, bring up the house lights, please." The acting secretary shielded his eyes with his hand, searching the crowd. "Jasper Simpson, come on down." The acting secretary chuckled after his poor impression of Bob Barker and turned to the president, apparently expecting a smile, but only receiving a stern look in response. He immediately turned to his subordinate, who was standing nearby, and whispered through a tight jaw. "Get Simpson up here, you idiot; the president is waiting. Where is he?"

The assistant turned to his assistant and said, "Where's Simpson, you idiot?"

The assistant to the assistant said, "I don't know. I never met the guy. You think he's here?"

"What do you mean? Do I think he's here?" said the assistant. "He's getting a damn award from the president. He damn well better be here."

The assistant to the assistant hesitated, looked at the president while the rest of the assistants stood looking at the floor or the ceiling, then walked to the podium, covered the microphone with his hand and said in the meekest of voices, "Excuse me, sir," smiled politely, and turned to the microphone. "And now, Mister Simpson, if you will come forward and receive your award."

There was a hush over the room as everyone strained in their chairs to see who would rise to the occasion. Boog felt the sweat trickling down the crease in his back. His legs felt weak, and the peppermint mousse he had just consumed started to churn in his stomach. It was too late to slide under the table, and as the seconds ticked away, he could feel his tie tightening and his face reddening as his heart pounded so loud within his chest he thought those around him at the table might feel the vibration.

Slowly, he began the process of making his legs lift his body from the chair. He felt his pants sticking to the seat from his sweat and imagined everyone gasping at the sight of his wet pants as he ascended the stage. When he finally stood, looking up at the podium and locking eyes with the president, the room burst into applause. Cheers erupted with elated pandemonium, and everyone slapped him on the back, attempted to shake his hand, and pushed him toward the steps to the stage. Marty stood at the top of the steps, holding her hand out to receive him as he advanced.

"Congratulations, Mister Simpson," she said as she grasped his hand and led him behind those on the stage who were standing and applauding, to stand next to the president.

The applause began to dissipate, and the president stepped closer to the microphone. "I guess you are not familiar with the phrase 'Never keep the president waiting.'" He laughed, looking at the audience, and they took the cue, offering spontaneous laughter as well. "Well, Mister Simpson, I am proud to meet you and know that everyone in this room, and across this country is proud of what you have done." The president looked at the acting secretary with a questioning glance, obviously unaware of what Boog had done to deserve the award. The acting secretary cupped his hand and whispered into the president's ear, and after the pause, the president continued. "I understand you are a hero of sorts back home. Where is it?"

"Hinkley County, sir."

"And you saved the school? That's quite something, yes indeedy." The president turned to the audience and raised his hands, clapping, and the assemblage once again erupted into applause.

Boog leaned toward the president as the commotion began to diminish and cupped his hand over his mouth. "It wasn't—I mean, I didn't really save the school," he said, pausing. "I just cleaned up a broken thermometer in the biology lab."

The president hastily placed his hand over the microphone, smiling at the crowd without turning his head and said, "Son, let's just keep that between you and me." Removing his hand, he leaned toward the microphone. "Folks, let's hope none of you are ever up against it like, like, uh—" he turned to Boog with a pleading look, having forgotten his first name.

"Boog, my name's Boog," he responded quietly.

"You mean, like Booger?" he said incredulously. The question echoed through the hall. The president smiled at the crowd and continued, "Let's hope none of you ever have to face the danger, uh, like Booger here had to, but if you do, remember—the full faith and power of the federal government is only one call away.

We will be there, looking over your shoulder, ready to defend the American way of life, freedom, and democracy." The president took Boog's hand, once again raising their joined hands in a sign of solidarity, and waved at the crowd with his other hand. The applause was deafening as the crowd rose for a standing ovation.

Boog felt himself being pulled from behind, and one of the black-suited security men stepped in front of him and next to the president, escorting him off the stage while the smiles and hand-waving continued. Boog was left standing behind the podium next to the acting secretary who was holding the engraved plaque, both watching as the crowd was shoved and parted by black-suited security men making a path for the president. The acting secretary turned with a stern look and shoved the plaque into Boog's hand.

"Here, *Booger,*" he said, emphasizing the name and turned to the assistant acting secretary. "That ought to play well in the papers tomorrow," he said rubbing his forehead and shaking his head. "None of you gave any thought to the fact that we were giving an award to a country hick named Booger?"

Marty stepped to the podium and took Boog by the hand, and they maneuvered through the standing dignitaries to exit the stage as the acting secretary brought the standing crowd to attention for his closing comments. Hands were shoved at Boog for quick shakes as they walked through the tables and he was slapped on the back so many times he thought his shoulder would become dislocated. They reached the back of the room and gave one last look at the disorderly crowd as the acting secretary formally ended the program.

Marty said, "Let's go before we get trampled by everyone heading for the bar. There's a private bar in my suite. I'm sure you could use some quiet time." She grasped his hand and pulled him toward the elevator.

• • •

Her suite was large and elaborately decorated with fine furniture, including a couch and large, overstuffed chair. The soft lighting enhanced the warmth of the room and Marty dimmed them further as she closed the door. She guided him to the couch and said, "Now, relax while I get us something to drink. What would you like?"

"Water would be fine." Boog pulled at his tie wishing he had scissors, as there seemed to be no way to release the tight knot.

"Are you sure just water? I can get you just about anything. Ten-year-old scotch, aged bourbon, Russian vodka—let's see—cabernet, chardonnay, there's even some champagne here."

"Uh, water will be fine; I don't drink, you know, that stuff." He felt insecure, inhibited, and about ten other in-somethings that he could not name. The room was closing in, and Marty's scent, something between fresh roses and the stuff Stella put on his towels when she washed them, was making his nose twitch.

"Really? You don't drink? I thought, you know, westerners all drank. I mean, to excess. You know, like in the movies—the cowboy thing—everyone standing at the bar, swilling down shots, and spitting. Well, maybe not the spitting anymore. So you don't drink. Don't tell me you're a vegetarian, do yoga, stuff like that?" Marty popped the cork of the chardonnay and poured some, holding up the glass and inspecting the contents in the dim light as if she were looking for bugs or other foreign matter.

"I'm not a vet-narian; I don't even have a pet. I had a turtle once, but when I moved over the hardware store, it got real cold one night, and the next day he didn't move, so I flushed him down the toilet. I don't drink because a good friend told me not to. He said spirits have no meaningful benefit for the soul. It might make your body feel good, for a while, but when it wears off, you are right back where you started."

Marty stared at him, trying to fathom the response to her question. Could he really not know what a vegetarian is? Could the person she thought cute, sensitive, and fashionably naïve, actually be flat-out ignorant? Could he be the hick the acting secretary referred to—a real country bumpkin? She decided to change the subject and challenge his intellect at another level. She moved to the couch and sat down, lounging in the plush cushions holding her wine glass at a vexing tilt next to her face, looking at him, still perplexed. "How did you save the school? Not that it's important to me." She nodded her head toward the plaque conspicuously sitting on the edge of an end table. "That's a pretty nice award, not to mention who presented it. So, what happened?"

"Well, that's the funny thing. Nothing really happened. Someone told me to go to the school; I don't even remember who told me. It might have been Stella. Anyway, someone told me to go to the school and clean up a mess in the biology lab. I suppose they called me because I'm the janitor at the courthouse and have experience with that kind of stuff. I mean messes—you know—somebody throwing up or spilling something sticky. Anyway, I went over to the school—it's just around the corner, remember, where the helio-copter picked you up. Anyway, I went to the school and cleaned up a broken thermometer—one of those with the cardboard backing. This one had a picture of a girl with long legs pumping gas, 'cause it was from Bud's Sunoco. Anyway, I cleaned it up before the folks from Cougar Falls could use all of their fancy equipment. In the end, I guess everyone was happy, everyone except the kids at the school, because they thought school would be cancelled. That's about it. Like I said—it really wasn't nothin'." He took a swallow of his fancy bottled water, leaned back, and started to feel relaxed for the first time since the evening began.

"Let me get this straight," Marty said with some authority, sitting up a little and placing her wine glass on the table. "You're the janitor at the courthouse. I mean, the real janitor—the guy that cleans the toilets and sweeps the floors?"

Boog smiled, feeling good about being recognized for his work and title. "That's me, the one and only. I take care of the whole building—interior and exterior. And I'm told," he said, sitting up with growing self-confidence and a hint of modesty, "you can travel all over the state and not find a cleaner courthouse."

This explanation of events, disclaimer, and proclamation of self-satisfaction at being a janitor was more unbroken words than Marty had ever heard from Jasper, or Boog, or whatever. Her imagined hero from the hinterland continued to crash and burn with each enriched definition of lifestyle and profession. He was a janitor, a guy that cleaned toilets, sitting here in an executive suite of the Hyatt Regency, drinking ten-dollar French bottled water after accepting presidential accolades for cleaning up a broken thermometer. No wonder the federal government was so screwed up.

Marty rose from the couch with an unsettled feeling that she needed to rethink her priorities and choice of evening companion. Then she looked at the hunk of testosterone holding down the other end of the couch and thought, *What the hell. He leaves tomorrow,* and sat back down on the couch with a plunk, picked up her wine glass, took a big swig and said, "Sose, what y'all do down there on the farm on Saturday night? Is it true what they say about sheep?"

• • •

Two Perrier's later, Boog's bladder was on overload, and Marty's questions concerning life in Hinkley County were growing less inquisitive and more sublime by the minute. She had completed the first bottle of chardonnay and was bracing herself against the wet bar, attempting to uncork the second bottle, spewing expletives as she berated whoever invented the corkscrew. Boog stood and announced it was time to leave.

"Leave?" Marty said with a start, slurring badly, losing her balance, and slamming the bottle down on the bar. "You can't leave now. I mean, don't you want to, to stay for a while? Uh, how about a movie? You think sheep are fun—wait until you see some of this stuff." She straightened and balanced herself and then made a move toward the television cabinet, but immediately lost her balance again and began to tilt toward the couch. Boog caught her arm as she slumped and led her to a soft landing. "Oh, Booger, my head is, is swimming. I think I—maybe I had too much wine. I'm kind of sick, I think." With the last comment lingering on her lips, she closed her eyes. "Oh, Boooo— Whoa, I've got to open my eyes." She tried to sit up, but the effort failed. "Oh, Booger, I don't feel so good."

After an hour of Marty sleeping with her head against his thigh, Boog finally made a move and carefully placed a pillow under Marty's head. He quietly made his way to the door and left the room.

Entering his own room, he was greeted by a blinking red light on his house phone, indicating he had messages. The cell phone he had left on the desk was blinking, indicating he had voice mail, and an envelope had been slipped under his door. After reading the instructions on the house phone, he finally retrieved the voice message from Stella: "Boog, where are you? I called your cell phone four times. I'm sorry I hung up on you before. Please call me and let me know what is happening. Well, I guess I'll go. I love you. I hope you are having a good time. Oh, yeah, and I will be at the airport tomorrow. I can't wait to see you."

He had no idea how to get the cell phone to quit blinking, so he put it in his suitcase. He opened the envelope and found a typed note.

Mr. Simpson, Ms. Stella is trying to reach you. She wishes you to call her as soon as possible. She has requested our security people search for you, but we are unable to do that unless there is an emergency. She has called our desk five times. Please call her at your earliest opportunity so she will stop calling here. Concierge desk.

He retrieved the cell phone, and after consulting the instructions left by Stella, dialed her number and pressed send.

"Hello." Stella's voice was full of sleep but soon erupted into full volume. "Boog, is that you? It's four-thirty in the morning. Where have you been? Don't tell me you have been at the banquet all this time."

He held the phone out to talk and to offer some relief from the screeching transmission. "Well, no, I haven't been at the banquet all this time. Is everything all right at home?" His concern didn't seem to sway her mood.

"Where you been then 'til this hour in the mornin'? And let me warn you, if you say you've been with that girl, you better find another ride home from the airport."

Uh-oh. Things were spiraling out of control way too fast, and telling a lie was not something he could easily do. As a child, any time he tried to cover even the most minor misdeed with a fib, he was caught like a catfish out of water. He decided to lay his cards on the table. The worst that could happen was a long hitchhike home. "Stell, I know this might not sound, you know, real good."

"What do you mean, real good? I'll tell you what's good and what ain't good. So spill it."

"Well, see, I got an award from the president, I mean the real president, the one that lives here. He gave me an award in front of the whole audience. It's real nice, it says—" then he realized he had left the plaque in Marty's room. "Well, it says some stuff about how I saved the school and stuff. Anyway the president—"

Stella's tone had decreased several decibels. "The president of the United States gave you another award, at the banquet, in front of everyone?"

"Well, yeah, right at the end, after dinner, they called my name, like I won the door prize, kind of like at the Legion hall or somethin', and I went on the stage and the president shook my hand and said some stuff. He kind of told me to keep quiet. And that was it." He listened into the phone, but all he heard was Stella breathing.

"Damn, Boog. No wonder you were out so late—probably celebrating. Damn. The president of the United States shook your hand and gave you an award." She was silent again, and he was about to proceed with the remainder of the story about how he ended up in Marty's room and his proclamation of innocence when she said, "I'll bet you'll be in the Sunday paper—maybe even on the TV. Damn, Boog, I'm so proud of you. I wish I were there to give you a big kiss. I wish I had been there to see you and the president. Was he friendly? That's okay; you can tell me all about it on the way home. I'll be at the airport, meet you where you get off the plane. I'm going to dream about you all night—well, at least for the next hour. Don't forget your award. Don't forget, you need to be at the airport at least two hours before you leave. Don't forget your gum. Call me from the airport before you take off, and don't forget I love you. You still there?"

"Uh, yeah, I'm still here. See you tomorrow, or later today, I guess." He closed the phone, put it in the suitcase, closed the lid, and blew out a big breath.

•••

The phone buzzed and aroused him from a deep sleep. It seemed as if he had just closed his eyes. Rolling over to answer the phone, he noted that he *had* just closed his eyes; it was five thirty. The phone buzzed again. "Hello."

"Mister Simpson, this is Richard Stein, NBC news. I'm the assistant producer for the *Today Show*. We would like to do a short interview with you. We understand you received an award from the president last night. Anyway, we would like to do a remote from the hotel there; let's see, it would be in the last hour, at eight-forty-seven—only about two and a half minutes. We can set you up in the lobby. Okay? Our local affiliate, channel seven will be there."

"What? Who are you? A remote what?" Boog rubbed his eyes. "Uh, I don't know what you want, but I have to go home today, so I don't have time."

"Our crew will be in the lobby. You should be in place no later than eight-thirty so the soundman can get levels and get you connected, and let's see, the site director needs to instruct you on camera placement. That should do it. Don't wear anything blue. Light and dark contrast is best, you know, white shirt and dark pants or a dark suit with a red tie, that kind of thing. No gum. It's best not to wear glasses, although that's up to you. That should do it. Oh, yeah, bring whatever they gave you. We might want to get a shot, although we probably won't have you hold it, but that's up to the site director. No later than eight-thirty, okay? Okay." The line went dead.

Boog sat on the side of the bed holding the phone. "What? Hello? Who are you?" There was no answer. He got up and stretched, looked at the phone again, and dismissed the call as just another practical joke. He searched for the livery service card and called, requesting Roger, and was advised that request could not be guaranteed, but that his pickup had already been scheduled for eight-forty-five. It was close to six, so there was no use going back to bed.

After showering and packing the few items he had taken out of his grip, he made the trek back to Marty's suite to retrieve his plaque. He lightly knocked on the door, but was not received. The second knock showed greater urgency and was eventually answered. The door opened a crack, stretching the security chain to its full length.

"Booger, uh, what do you want? You know it's only seven o'clock?" From what he could see through the crack, Marty was not an early riser and not fond of pajamas, either. "God, my head hurts. Hold on a minute." She closed the door, and a minute later, he heard the security chain released and the door opened. She had put a robe on but still blocked entrance to her room. "Look, Boog, or whatever, I really don't feel very good, and well, whatever I said or did last night, just forget it, okay? I had a little too much wine. We both know that. I'm sorry if I hurt your feelings." With one hand still on the door, she bent over and covered her mouth with the other hand. She lost the color in her face and made a desperate, almost falling dash for the bathroom. Boog caught the door as it closed and stepped in. He heard her retching in the bathroom and casually walked over and retrieved his plaque.

Stepping up to the closed bathroom door, he said, “You okay?”

“Leave me alone,” she said between spits.

“Hope you get to feelin’ better. Ralph—he owns Ralphy’s at home—he always said that if you put a raw egg in a glass, mix it with a little warm beer and swallow it in one gulp, it’d cure a hangover right away.” Marty belched another dry heave. “Yeah, well, might not work the same for everyone. Okay, see ya.”

• • •

Plaque in one hand and suitcase in the other, he scanned the room one last time before departing. Opening the door, he almost bumped into Roger, who was raising his hand to knock. “Hey, Roger.”

“Hey, Goob. Ready to rock and roll?” Roger reached for Boog’s suitcase. “Hey man, that’s a nice award. That yours?”

“Yeah, the president gave it to me.”

“No shit. You talkin’ the big guy, numero uno, the commander and chief?” Roger took the plaque and examined it. “What’d you do? Man, you some kind of hero. Way to go, Goob.”

A young lady dressed in blue jeans, a sweatshirt with an NBC peacock emblem embroidered on the front, and a headset on her head with an unattached cord dangling from it came up behind Roger. “Mister Simpson, I presume; I’m Linda Weatherby, Channel Seven News. If you will follow me, we’ll go downstairs and get set up. The camera crew and sound man are waiting to get the shot.” She glanced at her watch. “We’ve got about twenty minutes, so we’re good.”

Boog looked at the young lady without response, then at Roger and said, “I guess they want to take my picture, but we don’t have time.” He turned to Linda. “We’re just leavin’ for the airport, so thanks anyway. Come on, Roger.” He put the plaque under his arm and turned toward the elevators with

Roger walking behind with the orange and brown fake straw color suitcase with a fake bone handle.

"Wait," Linda shouted, franticly running ahead and blocking the hall. "You can't just leave; the *Today Show* has you scheduled," she glanced again at her watch, "in seventeen minutes." She backed down the hall in front of them as they moved toward the elevator, raising her hand, palm out. "Now, let's all just calm down, get on the elevator, and go downstairs. This will only take a few minutes. You won't be late for wherever you are going." Her face brightened. "You scheduled to be on one of the other morning shows? I bet it's *The View*, isn't it? They call this morning?" Her cell phone chortled an unfamiliar song. "Yeah," she answered, still backing in front of them. "We're on our way down. They're in a hurry—supposed to be at another studio, *The View*. Yeah, I should have guessed, too." She closed the phone, turned, and pressed the down button. "Okay, Jasper, show time."

They stood in the elevator, Roger still holding the suitcase. "Goob, you gonna be on the *Today Show*? Damn, man. You are some kind of hero. Damn, this be cool as hell. I wish my old lady was here; she really digs that dude that does the weather."

The door opened, and Linda grabbed Boog's arm and pulled him, rushing toward the atrium lounge area of the hotel lobby. There were several technicians, a man holding a television camera, another holding a big boom microphone, and another well-dressed woman holding a makeup kit. Linda pushed him to a position in front of the camera and signaled for the makeup girl to take over. She stepped back and plugged her headset into a port on the cameraman's backpack and began talking.

"Now just relax while I get rid of any shiny spots on your face." The makeup lady raised a brush toward his face, and Boog took a step back, tripping over a planter and almost falling into the fountain. A technician grabbed his arm and lifted him back into position. "It's okay, dear; I'm not going to hurt you. It's just some powder to soften your facial oil."

Boog frantically looked around for Roger. “Roger, where’d you go? Tell ‘em we’re gonna be late.”

Roger stepped up behind him and quietly said, “We got time, Goob. Just relax, man. This is the *Today Show*. You on national TV.”

“Okay, but stand right there. Don’t go anywhere.”

Linda shouted, “Five minutes to air.” The makeup girl ruffled his shirt collar and ran a lint brush down the front of his coat while a technician fitted an earpiece and strategically placed a small microphone inside his jacket.

The makeup girl turned to Linda. “Probably want to go with a torso shot; I can’t do anything with the pants—the hair, either—not enough time.” She turned to go behind the camera. “Maybe if I had a month.”

“Okay, let’s get set. Mister Simpson, we need to get a sound check. Just give us a few words.” Boog looked like a deer caught in high beams. “Uh, how about just counting to ten,” she said in a disgusted tone.

He turned and looked at Roger for help. “Just start counting,” Roger whispered from behind a palm frond next to Boog.

“Uh, one, two—”

“A little louder please,” Linda demanded. “Two minutes to air. Keep counting.”

“Uh, three, four, five.” He turned and looked at Roger. “I think I’m gonna be sick.”

“No, man, you ain’t gonna get sick. Just smile that big farm boy smile, and, and act naturally, like that singer Buck Owensby sang.”

“Who?”

“Buck Owensby or Owens or something. He had this song—“Act Naturally.” Oh, never mind.”

One of the technicians stepped up and held a flat screen TV monitor next to the camera lens. On the monitor, Boog saw people sitting on a couch, talking. There was a crackle in his earpiece, and then he could hear the people that were sitting on the couch, laughing and talking about their next guest, Jasper Simpson.

"One minute to air." Linda came over to Boog and straightened his shoulders toward the camera. "Could you hear the hosts through your ear piece?" Boog nodded his head. "Okay, they're in commercial break right now. I will go back to the camera, but I'll be looking right at you. I will count down to air time with my fingers, like this." She held up her hand and counted down from five with her fingers. "When I get to one, the red light on the camera will go on. You look right at the camera. You will be able to see the host in that monitor, but you need to look into the camera. She will say hi, introduce you, and then ask you a question or two—you know, what's it like down on the farm, stuff like that."

"I don't live on a farm. I live in a trailer."

"Wow, now there's a factoid I never would have guessed. Anyway, just answer the questions, or say anything you want. We're scheduled for two and half minutes. That doesn't sound like much, but it's a lifetime on live TV." She put her hand up to her earphone and spoke to no one. "Okay, got it. All right, we're thirty seconds out. I'm going to step back. Just watch my fingers."

Boog turned and looked at Roger, standing just out of camera view. Roger smiled and gave him the two-fingers up peace sign. He looked back at Linda, and she gave him the two-finger peace sign. Then the one finger sign, and then the red light went on.

"Now we have with us Jasper Simpson from—let's see, Hinkley County, Illinois. Is that right, Jasper? And where is Hinkley County?"

Boog stared at the red light, but said nothing.

"Uh, can you hear me, Jasper? Maybe we have a bad signal." The host looked off-camera for a sign that there might be a problem. "Can you hear me now?"

Before the technician standing just out of camera could stop him, Roger reached over and jabbed Boog in the arm. "Speak up, man. She axed you a question." The technician grabbed Roger and pushed him away.

Linda was waving her arms, pointing at the camera lens, and then pointing at her mouth.

"Okay, they say we have a good signal now. Jasper, can you hear me? Tell me about meeting the president. I assume it was your first time."

Boog continued to stare at the red light. Finally, Linda walked toward him, as close as she could get without blocking the camera and whispered. "Talk, you idiot."

He opened his mouth and tried to form words, and then started counting again. "One, two, three, uh, four—"

"Go to black, go to black," Linda said, sinking to the floor on her crossed legs and holding her head.

The host's face filled the monitor. "Well, unfortunately, there seems to be some technical difficulties down at the Hyatt. Maybe we can get things straightened out when we come back from this break. This is *Today*, on NBC." The monitor faded to black and then came back up with the host turning to someone standing off-camera. "Who arranged that? You may as well have had a cow standing there for me to talk to."

Roger walked over to Boog, shaking his head. "Man, that was about the most pathetic thing I've ever seen. Man, you froze up. Let's get out of here."

The technician came over and viciously ripped the earpiece and microphone off Boog. Linda raised her head from her hands and looked at him. "What kind of moron counts on live national TV? They send me an idiot and expect to do an interview. Well, it's not my fault."

Chapter 18

Stella rushed around her small house, attempting to get her kids dressed and fed before taking them to her mother's. On normal mornings, she watched the *Today Show* until she left for work, but this morning, her youngest had SpongeBob blaring musical lyrics while he ingested fruit loops in front of the TV. She ran through the room, almost jumping over the boy, stopping only when she realized he wasn't dressed. "Baby, you need to get dressed; Mommy's late, and you have to go to Grammy's." She grabbed the remote and shut the TV off, lifting the boy to his feet, giving him a love pat on the butt, and urging him to hurry and get dressed. The phone rang, causing her to dish out an expletive and then look up, cross herself, and ask for divine forgiveness for her verbal indiscretion.

"Stella, that you? Stella, turn on the TV. Hurry." It was her mother.

"My God, what's wrong? Don't do this to me. It's not a plane crash or something, is it? I don't have time, Mom."

"Turn on the damn TV, now; the *Today Show*. It's Jasper Simpson; he's gonna be on TV as soon as this commercial is over."

"Oh, my God." Stella threw down the receiver and ran to the remote. She punched the on button and waited for the picture to appear. SpongeBob was still bubbling. She switched the channel and waited for a vaginal itch cream commercial to end.

"And now we have Jasper Simpson—"

Stella's jaw dropped as she stood face to face with Boog, only he was on the TV screen. The picture went back and forth, Boog staring at her, back to the host suggesting there were technical difficulties, and then back to Boog, mute, staring at her, back to the host saying, "Can you hear me?" And then there was Boog, counting, "Uh, one, two, three—"

"Oh, honey, you poor baby," was all she could say. "But, you look so handsome in that new coat."

• • •

As they rode toward the airport, he could hear Roger talking to his wife. “Did you see me? That was my hand that punched him in the arm. Technical difficulties, my ass. No, he just froze up, like a big icicle.”

Boog sat in the back, holding his plaque, watching the traffic, thinking about the boiler room, Stella, and what Tug would have said about all of the clutter that was gathering in his life.

Roger yelled back, “Hey, Goob, you okay? Don’t let that thing back at the hotel get you down. You’re one of the good guys, not like those honkies that think they run the country. You still a hero, no matter what. And you got the award that says so.”

“Roger, we have time to pull over for a minute?”

“What, you got to pee or something? Yeah, we got time. Another ten minutes, we’ll be at the airport, and your plane doesn’t leave for another hour.”

“Just pull over, there, where that crick runs next to the highway.” Boog pointed ahead and to the right.

“Man, you can’t pee right out here next to the highway. I’ll get a ticket sure as hell.”

“I don’t have to pee. Just pull over.” Roger continued to slow, eventually grinding to a halt on the shoulder. Boog opened the door as Roger stepped out and came around the limo. The traffic speeding by created such turbulence that Roger’s hat blew off and he had to run to retrieve it.

Returning with his hand on his hat, holding it in place, he yelled, “What we stopped here for?”

Boog stood for a moment, looking at the stream of water running next to the highway shoulder; it was full of flotsam—Styrofoam cups, broken plastic car parts, paper, and an occasional chunk of tire—and without hesitation, flung the award plaque into the stream and said, “Let’s go.”

“What you do that for? Damn, man, the president give you that.”

Boog turned, got back into the limo, and closed the door.

Roger got back behind the wheel and blended back into traffic. Shaking his head, he said, "You farm boys sure got some funny ways about you. And that sheep thing—is that true?"

• • •

As he walked up the jet way, his mood mellowed with each step toward the entrance into the terminal. The solitude of the flight had given him time to review the events of the previous two days as well as the past few months. The momentum of his advancement to his current position and all that followed, including undeserved accolades and awards, had changed his life. Instead of being an observer of the less-than-dramatic, and for the most part, uninteresting Hinkley County limelight, he was now the observed, the person that garnered the attention and created the limelight.

Tug Longwater had instilled a basic life lesson early in their relationship. Rather than languish in self-pity and misery, take whatever steps are necessary to face the adversity and correct the direction of your life. Boog's epiphany while relaxing in the comfort of his first-class leather reclining seat on the airplane was that he was never happier than the day preceding his meeting with the commissioners and their decision to promote him to director of homeland security. And he had never been unhappier than when he entered the aircraft he had just exited. It was time to take whatever steps were necessary, as Tug would put it, to make things right.

Stella ran to him as he stepped into the terminal. "Hey, Stell," was all he could get out before she wrapped her arms around his neck and kissed him over and over. The other passengers walked around them, overlooking the inconvenience, given the exuberant emotional display.

"Oh, honey. I missed you so much. And that thing on TV—I felt so sorry for you. They should have told you they were going to turn the camera on. It doesn't matter; you looked so handsome standing there with your award, the one the president gave you. Where is it? I can't wait to see it. I bet it's made out of gold or silver or something." She hugged him again. "Come on, let's go get your suitcase, and then you can tell me all about your trip and the banquet, and I just can't believe you were on the *Today Show*." She looked around at the crowd, looped her arm through his, and loudly said with a beaming smile, "He was on the *Today Show* this morning. He received an award from the president of the United States."

A few people looked their way, more out of curiosity at why a plainly dressed country girl would be yelling at them than at the meaning of her statement, but then several people clapped their hands in recognition, and there were a few whistles before everyone went about their business, rushing to their next destination.

Once they were settled into the car, the questions spewed from Stella's mouth like water over Niagara Falls. Boog didn't really feel like talking, but was forced to recall most of the details of his trip, although he tried to avoid some of the specific questions like, "Is your award in your suitcase?" "Where did you go to celebrate?" And the big one, "Tell me again why that girl was in your room when I called." He managed to change the subject whenever necessary, and Stella, the excitement of the TV appearance still in the forefront, seemed to roll with the conversation.

The big issue that he did not broach in the conversation was the fact that he had decided to divest himself of his position, appeal to the commissioners to reinstate his singular janitorial duties, move back to his room above the hardware store, and restore the simplicity of his life that he had once enjoyed. He knew this would be a shock and disappointment to Stella, whom he assumed was attracted to him because of his celebrity and not his personality or appearance. After all, they had been acquaintances for many years, and only recently had she shown any desire to communicate beyond the occasional request to clean up a mess in the courthouse.

Arriving at the trailer, Stella jumped out of the car and immediately stuck her head back in the car saying, "You stay right here. Don't get out until I come out and get you." She closed the car door and ran to the trailer, climbing the steps and slamming the door behind her. Boog stared out the window at the big yellow Hummer that seemed to be saying, "What's the matter, little boy? The pressure too much?" A minute later, she came out, opened his door, and grabbed his hand. "Come on, I've got a little welcome home surprise for you."

He stepped up to the trailer door, and she pushed him ahead, hefting the suitcase as she followed. Inside, the trailer was adorned with lighted candles and soft mood music; the dining table was set with glass dinnerware, silverware, and wine goblets. The aroma of roasted something wafted from the up-to-now unused oven, and as he looked down the hall, he saw a big, red, heart-shaped pillow with white tapestry on the bed proclaiming *I love you.* The bed linens were folded back in an inviting fashion and additional candles flickered at the bedside.

"Now, you sit down while I get dinner ready. Mom has the kids for the night and tomorrow, bein' it's Saturday, we don't have to be anywhere or do anything, so I am going to make you happy to be home. I know you probably got some big ideas, bein' in Washington and seeing all of the sights and all, but I think it's time we have an understanding that this is where you belong—here and with me." She flitted around the small area, opening canned vegetables and other delicacies, turning to Boog every few minutes with a smile saying, "I'm sure glad you are home," or "I missed you so much."

•••

Saturday morning, Boog awoke from a deep sleep with his arm draped across Stella. The perpetual smile Stella had worn all evening had relaxed into contentment as she lay beside him, murmuring in her sleep. That smile had now somehow affixed itself to his face. He lay on his back, the big heart pillow on top of him, smiling, trying to remember why he was so unhappy the day before. Stella cooed, moved closer, and nestled her head in the crook of his arm. The thought that maybe he would delay any rash decision to quit or relinquish his position seemed to hover among the many other pleasant feelings that stirred his emotions as he lay next to Stella.

Stella moved a little, laid her arm across his chest, and whispered, "Hey, Boog."

"Hey, Stell."

"I love you."

This was a position he had never been in before. Everything about it was foreign. The crowded bed, a girl in the bed making it crowded—him, in the crowded bed, with the girl. How do I respond? She keeps saying that love stuff and waiting for a response.

Stella broke the silence. "The first thing we are going to do this morning is go to your office and hang your plaque. I never did see it last night. I got so excited after dinner, I forgot all about it. Anyway, I don't have to pick the kids up until noon, so we can have breakfast, or do anything you want." With that comment, she twirled her finger in the hair on his chest and grinned from ear to ear.

Boog stared at the ceiling and said, "Well, see, I kind of lost the plaque."

Stella sat up, pulling the sheet around her. "What do you mean 'you lost it'? You don't lose something the president of the United States gives you." She slumped back down on the bed, staring at the ceiling as well, shaking her head. "Okay, let's hear it. I might as well get used to this. Sometimes, Boog, I forget that you are—well, Boog. Honey, I don't mean that in a bad way. I mean—It doesn't matter. Just tell me what happened to the damn plaque."

He proceeded to tell her the story of the TV interview fiasco and the trip to the airport, trying to describe how he felt and why he threw the plaque in the creek. When he finished, he was pretty satisfied that he had plead his case with some semblance of rational order and reasoning.

Stella brought her hand down, slapping herself in the forehead. "What in the world were you thinking? The president shakes your hand and gives you an award, and you throw it in the crick by the side of the highway?"

Obviously, he had not made his point with the precision necessary to garner a sympathetic reaction. "Uh, it really wasn't that big of a plaque. Maybe we can go to the Sears store and get another one."

There was a knock on the trailer door, and Boog slid from Stella's grasp, modestly wrapping himself in a towel, and thankfully made his way out of the bedroom. "I'll see who that is."

Cracking the door, he found Red Redderson, the twice-weekly *Hinkley Messenger*'s editor, standing with one foot on the step, blowing warm breath into his cold hand. "Boog, how's it going? Congratulations, man. An award from the president; it doesn't get much better than that. Can I come in? I'd like to get some words of wisdom from our newest national hero. I've had calls from all over the country asking about you, wanting pictures and copy from the high school article. Can I come in? It's freezing out here. Hey, that your car? Somebody really did a number on it." Boog looked out to find Stella's car covered with what appeared to be cow manure. In addition, there was shaving cream on the windshield scrawling out the word "Retard."

"Uh, Red, it's not a good time right now."

Stella yelled from the back of the trailer, "Who is it?"

Red leaned to peek through the crack in the door, and Boog stepped forward to block his view. Red smiled and said, "Yeah, I guess it's not a very good time—at least, for an interview. How about I come back this afternoon? Or how about you call me? Here's my number." Red handed him a card and again tried to peek through the crack, without success. He shook his head and smiled. "Hero worship, right here in our little town. I'll be damned. Okay, call me when you have time," he said curtly with a hint of jealousy, and turned and walked away.

Boog again made a cursory examination of the car and closed the door. Stella walked up behind him in a robe she had apparently stashed while he was gone and again asked, "Who was that?"

"Red from the paper. Wants me to call him. I think I'll wait for a while." He looked at her, and then at himself, standing with a towel wrap, and suddenly felt extremely self-conscious. "Uh, I think I'll get dressed." He hurried to the back of the trailer and slid the pocket door shut.

Stella smiled and shook her head, reliving the evening before, how she had guided him through the lovemaking process, realizing he had never been intimate before. "Honey, did I hear something about a car?"

Being called honey was more than a little strange. He envisioned the smirks and chuckles from the courthouse staff when she yelled "Oh, honey" down the courthouse hall. "Well, there is a little problem with your car. I think Bud may have come around last night."

He heard the trailer door open and then slam shut. "That jerk; that miserable, drunken jerk. I am sick of him and his friends. I am not going to put up with it anymore." He could hear her throwing things. He peeked out of the door and saw she was retrieving her scattered clothing and getting dressed while she talked to herself.

He came out and stood looking at the wall or up at the ceiling, purposefully not looking at her while she dressed. "It's just Bud, trying to, you know, be funny or something. Don't worry about it. I'll talk to him again next time I see him. I'll wash your car today. There's a hose right out next to the trailer."

"Don't make excuses for him. He's a first-class jerk." She then said forcefully, "You will not wash that car. I am going to find him. I am going to make him clean my car and apologize in front of me and my children."

Boog stood somewhat sheepishly, still staring at the wall, since Stella was partially disrobed in her bra and panties.

"Aw, baby, I didn't mean to yell at you." She came to him and hugged him, obviously not self-conscious about her exposed body. "I promise I will never yell at you. I will never be like him, and I know you never will because you are the kindest, gentlest man I have ever met. I love you."

He gently hugged her back and thought, *There she said it again.*

• • •

The headline over Boog's high school graduation picture in the twice-weekly *Hinkley Messenger* declared, "Local DHS Director Hailed as Hero" with the following story under Red Redderson's byline.

The county Department of Homeland Security director, Jasper (Boog) Simpson was personally recognized by the president of the United States at the recent national meeting of the Department of Homeland Security held in Washington D.C. Simpson was recognized for his heroic action during a recent near disaster at the Hinkley High School after a toxic waste spill caused evacuation of the school. The commendation stated that Simpson's courageous and prompt action prevented personal injury and potentially serious environmental harm. The statement released by the White House praised Simpson for his organizational skills while setting up and running the local Department of Homeland Security. The statement went on to say the local department had met all federal criteria necessary to qualify for FEMA assistance in the event of a natural disaster and gives the county priority treatment when applying for any future federal grants. Simpson made a guest appearance on the nationally broadcast NBC Today Show *carried on local affiliate channel four, but technical difficulties interrupted the interview.*

The local department is under the direct control and supervision of the Board of County Commissioners. Chet Sadinski, president of the Board of County Commissioners said of Simpson, "The young man has really done an outstanding job. We chose Simpson over numerous other well-qualified candidates because we recognized his hidden talents and superior management capabilities." When asked if Simpson might be considered for promotion to any other county position in the future, Sadinski said he could not comment on county employment issues. Prior to being promoted to director of the local homeland security office, Simpson held the position of courthouse custodian for fifteen years. Simpson was unavailable for comment at press time.

Chapter 19

It was a mild Wednesday in March, and Boog toiled at his desk, trying to maneuver a tiny pinball into maximum point position in the hand-held pinball toy left by Stella's youngest child during their last visit to his office. He had almost mastered the necessary hand coordination to elevate his score past Stella's five-year-old son when the elevator opened, and Stella's clattering heels signaled her trot down the hall. She slid to a stop at the door, eyes bulging with excitement. "Hey, Boog."

"Hey, Stell."

"You are not going to believe what's in the parking lot. I mean, you will not believe this. It's, it's—" Her mouth continued to move, but she was apparently having difficulty verbalizing the description.

"A boat and a four-wheeler?" He moved the little plastic pinball toy sandwiched between his big hands a little to the right. "Darn it, I just about had it. Another hundred points and I would have beaten the record. Well, Eric's record. I'm not sure what the world record is, but I'm sure he's close." He looked up to see Stella staring at him, that womanly look that can only be described as shock, awe, and disgust, all rolled into one big blank stare.

"You know about the boat? You knew it was coming and—Wait a minute. How did you know about the boat?" She moved a little closer and put both hands on the desk, leaning toward him. "Put the toy down and explain to me how you knew some big freaking truck was gonna pull into our parking lot today with a boat and four-wheeler hanging on the back."

"They called and said it would be here today."

Stella sighed and shook her head, her large curls dangling over her face. "Sometimes, Jasper Simpson, you make it very difficult to control my temper. I try. Believe me; I try. Now, let's start over. Someone called. Who would that someone be?"

Uh-oh. Since returning from Washington, there had not been much conversation about Marty, which was just fine with him because it was not a pleasant topic. "Uh, it was someone from Washington, just letting me know the delivery date."

"Oh, would that someone be the same someone who came to your room in Washington? The same someone you never want to talk about in Washington?" Stella took a more composed and relaxed position, sitting on the edge of the desk with her arms crossed, waiting for a response.

"Well, yes, that would be the person that called," he answered hesitantly. Not a moment too soon, Chet Sadinski walked out of the commissioners' office and stood in the doorway, arms crossed.

"Anyone know what that semi is doing in the parking lot? He askin' for directions or something? Hell of a boat. Did you see it? Like something out of a cop movie, all decked out with emergency lights. Guess I'll go take a closer look before he leaves." Sadinski turned to walk toward the elevator.

"Mister Sadinski," Stella called. "Maybe you ought to discuss this with," she hesitated, "Mister Simpson." She gave Boog a stern look as she rose from the desk. "Meanwhile, I'll go see what the semi driver wants."

Sadinski interrupted his stroll toward the elevator and came back, passing Stella, giving a questioning stare, but got no response. "Booger, you know anything about this?" he said, watching Stella disappear into the elevator. "You know, she's a fine looking woman, in her own way." He continued to look at the empty hallway, obviously distracted, and then turned back to Boog. "So, do you know the driver or something?"

Sadinski's mood and attempt at casual conversation was surprising, and Boog searched for a way to keep the tone of the encounter light. "Well, no, I don't know the driver, but I do know where the boat and four-wheeler came from and where they're going."

Sadinski, leaning against the door jam, crossed his arms and waited for more information. "The assistant to the assistant from Washington called this morning and said they were sending some equipment to help us fight some more terrorism. I guess there are some terrorists moving this way or something, maybe over by Cougar Falls, I mean, it's not like we are, you know, under attack or anything."

Sadinski stared at him with a raised eyebrow.

"What in blazes are you talking about? Terrorists in Cougar Falls? I never heard about any terrorists. Booger, you been dreamin' or something. If I didn't know you better, I'd say you been in the wacky weed or something."

Boog could hear the slap of leather to the terrazzo floor moving at a fast pace. Ralph Bellows grabbed Sadinski's arm. "Terrorists? Where?" His red nose and cheeks flared as he drew breath and flailed his arms. "Did they blow up another building? Is it Chicago? Oh, no, not the Sears Tower. Was it the tower? Damn, we got to do something. Are they comin' this way?" He grabbed at his pants, pulling them up over his distended belly, slapped the palm of his hand to his forehead, and said, "I got to get home, get ready. How long we got?" Before Sadinski could reply, Bellows turned and rushed back toward the elevator.

"Ralph, calm down; there ain't no terrorists." But it was too late; he already was entering the elevator door, talking to himself. "Damn," Sadinski said. "Oh, well, by three o'clock this afternoon, he won't remember why he's so upset." He lingered, staring down the hall again, apparently gathering his thoughts, and turned back to Boog. "Now, let's start over. There's a semi down in the parking lot with a boat and a motor scooter on it. Where did it come from, and why is it here?"

Boog stared back at him, a momentary lapse, while he cleared his dry throat and muttered, "I ordered 'em from the catalogue those people left—the ones that brought the Hummer." Truth always made him feel better, no matter what the consequences.

Sadinski kept his steely gaze on Boog. "And?"

"And, that's it. She called and said the stuff would be here today. The part about the terrorists and stuff, well, she really didn't say that."

"Who's she?" Sadinski said, adding, "And it's free, like the Hummer and the trailer?"

Boog grinned, realizing he had struck a nerve with Sadinski. He leaned back in his chair with his hands clasped behind his head. "That's what she said, she being the assistant to the assistant. 'Order anything you want that'll help fight the terrorists and such,' is what she said."

"But we ain't got a lake, Booger; hell, we don't even have a river, 'cept the head water of the Olatagwa, and it pretty much dries up during the summer. Did you tell them that?"

Boog hesitated after that question. He didn't know he had to specify where they would hunt terrorists with the boat. Featherstone had a boat, and he must use it somewhere. "Well, not exactly. I mean, there wasn't any place on the order form to tell 'em where you was gonna use the boat. I just thought it looked pretty cool, all the lights and stuff, and it looked a lot like Mister Featherstone's bass boat."

"And it's free? You're sure?"

Boog vigorously nodded his head. "Well, I'll be damned. Let's go have a look."

And they did. The semi driver was winching the boat off the trailer when they walked out of the courthouse. Sheriff Minor was leaning against his SUV, watching, and rhythmically moving a toothpick from one side of his mouth to the other. When he saw Sadinski, he remarked, loud enough for the gathering crowd to hear without directing his comment to anyone in particular, "Nice boat. I wonder whose barn it will end up in. And that four-wheeler—I'm sure the taxpayers are happy we have one of those; that is, if they have a chance to see it before it disappears."

Sadinski fumed, trying to hold back any comment. He walked over and leaned against the SUV as well. "Busy day,

Sheriff, or you just taking a break after chasing all those illegal immigrants?"

Sheriff Minor pulled his toothpick out of his mouth, still looking at the driver toiling with the boat. "Just monitoring the county parking lot, Chet. Was gonna give this boy a ticket for double-parking 'til I found out he worked for you, so I cut him a break."

Sadinski continued to lean against the SUV, watching the driver, directing his comments to the sheriff without looking in his direction. "Big of you, Sheriff. I'm sure he appreciated it. But he doesn't work for me. You must be mistaken."

"Maybe. I guess we'll just have to wait and see who comes for this here boat and four-wheeler; then we'll know who he works for, won't we?" Minor put the toothpick back in his mouth, stood straight, stretched, and yawned. "Yep, we'll just have to wait. But in the meantime, I probably ought to put some chains on 'em, so they don't disappear before we find out, don't you think?" He pushed himself away from the vehicle, spit the toothpick on the ground next to Sadinski's foot, and strolled over to the activity near the boat. "Special Deputy Boog, you keep an eye on this here equipment until I can get some security chains attached, you hear? I wouldn't want it to float away, if you know what I mean." Stepping back, looking at the equipment in admiration, he continued, "My, my, that's some kind of boat. And I'll be—you see that? That four-wheeler has a trailer hitch, too. And it's all color-coordinated. Ain't that just special?" He turned and walked back toward his SUV, shaking his head and smiling. "Ooh, doggies, those feds really do know how to spend the money."

Sadinski had to step away from the vehicle as Sheriff Minor spun his wheels, exiting the parking lot without even a wave goodbye. Sadinski shoved his hands in his pockets and took one last look at the boat as Boog and the driver maneuvered it into a parking space, turned, and walked back toward the courthouse, mumbling.

Chapter 20

As spring approached, the courthouse parking lot looked a lot like a showroom display for the Department of Homeland Security. The trailer, Hummer, special edition police boat, and color-coordinated four-wheeler were all lined up, one after the other—bright and shining from Boog's once-a-week wash and wax. By the size of the chains securing the boat and four-wheeler and the tight grip Sheriff Minor maintained on the key ring for the Hummer, it had become obvious that unless there was a new "share the wealth" game plan concerning federal gifts, no one, including the commissioners, would benefit.

Boog and Stella had just enjoyed an early movie at the Cineplex and stopped at Ralphy's for a burger and Coke. Most of the patrons were eating, although the bar had a fare number of beer guzzlers starting their long Saturday night ritual. Stella slowly worked her way through a cheeseburger, and Boog devoured the Saturday night special. Neither paid attention to any other activity in the dining room, exchanging smiles and light conversation, mostly Stella's.

Taking a last sip on her straw, Stella looked around the room for the young lady waiting tables to request a refill. Her eyes met Bud's stare as he leaned with his back against the bar holding a beer bottle, his deep-set, darkened eyes evidence of a long day of drinking. His shirttail was half out, and his belly pushed against the buttons of his blaze-orange hunting vest. His John Deere ball cap was pulled down tight on his forehead, and his facial expression and body language announced "danger-*zone,*" cautioning the other bar patrons to give him a wide berth as he stood surveying the room.

Stella promptly said, "I'm ready to go. I can get a take-out container for the rest of my sandwich."

This came as a disappointment to Boog as he had readied himself for her offer to allow him to finish her sandwich as she had done so many times before. Rarely did he question Stella's request or motive, and this time was no different. He merely pushed his empty plate aside and rose to help her with her coat as she dug in her purse, searching for coinage for the tip. He could tell she was distracted, even nervous about something, but assumed she was worried about the late hour and her children. She pushed a few coins to the center of the table and briskly turned toward the exit. Boog fumbled with his coat as he tried to keep up with her, giving one last, longing look at her unfinished sandwich that, in her hurry, had obviously been forgotten.

"Gonna go do it with the retard?" Bud yelled from the bar as they reached the door. Stella stopped, not looking at Bud, holding her hand on the door, as if she was stunned by the remark. Boog stood behind her as a hush drew over the room. Stella slowly turned her head and looked at Bud, her distraught look drawing attention to the tears starting to run down her cheek. She took Boog's arm and pulled him through the door, and they heard Bud's boisterous voice as they exited. "Kinda follows her around like a puppy dog, don't he?"

Stella continued to pull Boog toward her car, which was parked down the street. By the time they reached the car, she was sobbing and forcefully said, "Get in. We are going home and tomorrow I am going to—I don't know—I'm going to do something. There has to be something."

Boog didn't get in the car, but walked her around to the driver seat and helped her get in. "You go ahead and go get your kids. I think I'll just walk back to the trailer. Don't worry about Bud; he's just all beered up." He touched her cheek where the moisture from a tear left a track. "I'll see you later, okay?" He walked back around the car and stood on the sidewalk, watching as she pulled into traffic, waving. Then he turned and walked back toward Ralphy's.

Bud still stood at the bar, facing away from the room now as Boog walked through the door. The crowd had grown louder with the encroaching late evening, and the bar was now full, with some patrons double-parked behind the occupied bar stools. Boog made his way through the tables to the bar and stopped when he reached Bud at the bar. Although the mirror behind the bar gave Bud a clear image of himself and Boog behind him, he apparently did not notice and continued to blankly stare at his near-empty beer bottle.

"Hey, Bud," Boog said flatly.

Bud turned and looked at him, then glanced around the room, apparently looking for Stella, before returning to meet Boog's stare. The alcohol-induced facial redness faded as he glared at Boog, but he said nothing.

"Bud, I think we need to talk. You got a minute?"

Bud tried to gather his composure, half turning to the bar and looking for recognition from the other patrons standing around him, but they either stared at their drinks or looked the other way.

"Uh, Bud? Maybe you didn't hear me." Boog raised his voice above the crowd noise. "I think we need to talk. Let's just step outside, where it's quiet, and we can straighten this out." A hush once again fell as the room came to attention. Bud turned to face the bar again and didn't say anything.

Ralphy walked down the inside of the bar and leaned against it on his elbow. "Bud, there's someone talking to you. Maybe you ought to take this outside."

Bud looked at Ralphy, and then looked into the mirror, seeing Boog standing behind him in the reflection. "Ain't got nothing to say to him, you, or anybody else in this town. You tellin' me I got to leave?" Bud's knuckles were white from gripping his empty beer bottle as he spoke.

"I'm telling you I don't want no trouble in here. You been spoutin' your mouth off, and enough's enough. Take it outside." Ralphy's stern voice implied that he meant business, and he continued to lean on the bar, waiting for Bud's reaction. Everyone knew Ralphy kept a dumb stick under the bar about where he stood for use on just such occasions. It was called a dumb stick because if you were dumb enough to cross Ralphy, you probably deserved a whack with the stick, which was a billy club about eighteen inches long with a leather strap through the handle.

Bud took his eyes from Ralphy and shot a glance in the mirror to see if Boog still had him blocked from behind, but Boog was gone. He turned, looked, and found no trace of Boog anywhere in the dining room. The confidence he had felt before the confrontation began to build, and he stepped back from the bar. He pulled at this cap and looked back at Ralphy. "I'm sure the beer is cold and my money is good someplace else. You ain't the only place in town, you know." Bud turned and swaggered toward the door. He took a brief glance through the diamond-shaped door glass and saw no one outside before exiting. He slid through the door and started toward his truck.

"Hey, Bud." Boog leaned against the front of Ralphy's with his hands in his pockets and jacket pulled up, fending off the cool spring dampness. Bud turned on his heels and stopped as Boog slowly walked toward him. "Bud, we need to get something straight. See, it doesn't bother me, you and the guys' sayin' stuff about me. I mean, I'm used to it. But Bud, I can't have you sayin' stuff about Stella or embarrassing her like you did in there. I know she was your wife and all, but it still ain't right. I guess I'm here to tell you, you got to stop. You understand?"

Bud stood erect, a couple inches taller than Boog with his cowboy boots on, and weaved slightly. His eyes were noticeably bleary. He smiled and said, "I understand, Boog. You're all in love and stuff. I understand." He stepped forward and held out his hand. "Let's shake on it."

Boog raised his hand, and Bud pulled back and sucker-punched him, catching him just to the right of his nose on his cheek. He really didn't feel much, but he heard the crunch of bone when the fist hit, and the force knocked him back, buckling his knees. He stumbled, but he did not lose his balance completely.

Boog raised his hand to his cheek, rubbed his nose checking for blood, and found none. "Ah, jeez, Bud, I wish you hadn't gone and done that."

Bud came forward and tried to kick Boog as he came upright, but Boog backed away and grabbed Bud's boot, twisting his leg and toppling him. Given the amount of beer Bud had in him and his lack of coordination, he went down hard on the cement and a rush of air left his lungs. Before he could turn over and try to get up, Boog put a knee in his back, pulled his arm around, and grabbed a handful of hair through his John Deere ball cap. As quick as the sucker-punch had started the fight, it was over. Bud lay with his face pressed against the cement sidewalk with Boog kneeling over him, holding Bud's arm behind his back and pressing his face down hard.

"Now, Bud, I want you to listen. This is very important. Are you listening?"

Bud gave a grunt.

Several people had come out of the restaurant, and several more had congregated along the sidewalk, watching.

"I didn't mean to hurt you, and I don't want to fight anymore. You understand?" Bud grunted again. "But if you ever talk that way again when Stella is around, or if she even tells me you talked to her in some nasty way, Bud, I will have to come find you, and well, it won't be pretty. You understand?" Bud didn't grunt or make a move. Boog lifted his head off the cement and said in a condescending way, "Bud, you listening to me?" And then said, very slowly, "Do you understand?"

Bud glanced through the corner of his eye at the crowd that had gathered and quietly said, "Whatever."

Chapter 21

The sun heated the cool spring air, and a light breeze ruffled the soiled curtains of the courthouse break room as Stella and Boog ate sandwiches she had prepared and brought from home. The daily lunch routine fit nicely into their blossoming relationship. Stella talked while Boog ate, relating the prior evening's adventure with her children or the new dress she was saving for, or the ever-constant problems with her car. What Boog lacked in communication skills he made up by being a great listener and sounding board for Stella's never-ending problems. And besides, with the exception of Tug Longwater, in his entire life, he had never had anyone that cared about him, prepared meals for him, took notice of his appearance, sometimes complementary and sometimes not, and generally accepted him for what he was, not for what they wanted him to be.

"They say there are supposed to be some storms this afternoon. Did you hear that? It doesn't look like it to me. It's beautiful outside. We could have gone out and sat on the bench in front, but I thought it might be too cold. Jasper Simpson, are you listening to me?" Boog looked up from his sandwich with a full mouth and vigorously nodded his head in the affirmative. "Bud called last night. Said he couldn't take the kids this weekend, again," she said with emphasis. "This is the third time in a row he has had some excuse. I thought we could do something this weekend, but he screwed up those plans.

"Do you ever think about going out of town, like a vacation—maybe to Chicago for the weekend? I haven't been out of this hick town, I don't know, since I was in high school and we took our spring trip to St. Louis to see the arch. Did you go? I don't remember seeing you. I didn't see much, other than Bud in those days. You know, we went up in the arch, it's like a long elevator ride, and then you have this long walk. Anyway, it was his big idea to try to find some closet or something to do it in up there. He wanted to come home and brag to his friends that he did it in the arch. I was stupid enough to go along with it, but luckily, when we did find what I think was a storage room or something, and Bud was trying to shove me in there, Mister Smithy saw him and that was the end of that adventure. And then, if you can believe this, Mister Smithy found Bud's stash of beer on the bus when we were leaving St. Louis and Bud got suspended for a week when we got home. He was lucky he got to graduate. Sometimes, Boog, I wonder what would have happened if I hadn't wasted my time with Bud. You know what I mean? If I had gone to college, maybe become a teacher—that's what I always dreamed I would be, a teacher—and helped with the cheerleading squad, like Misses Rogers. You remember her?" Stella had been looking out the window as she talked, and when she turned to look at Boog, his eyes were shut, and he was leaning back against the wall. Stella sighed and said to herself, "Oh, well," and started cleaning up the table in preparation to return to the information desk.

• • •

Early in the afternoon, the skies began to darken and the horizon took on an ominous appearance with deep purple thunderheads punctuated by red and yellow strands of beaming sunlight. Occasional far-off rumbles of thunder gave prelude to what the forecasters had predicted to be a potentially unstable and dangerous situation that could lead to tornado producing conditions.

The National Weather Service issued weather alerts every time a thunderstorm announced itself, so when the storm alert blared in the sheriff's office, Marge Stopher, designated day dispatcher, record keeper, jailhouse matron, and office manager walked over and hit the off button. She did have the foresight to follow the most used acronym in the office, CYA (cover your ass) by radioing Sheriff Minor, who was returning from the state capital after the Fraternal Order of Police state convention, and advising him that the alert had come across the weather radio. She told him it was the lowest category, a storm watch, and that from her window it just looked like another spring thunderstorm. He said he would be back in the office within the hour.

For the past five years running, the National Weather Service had issued proclamations about the effectiveness of storm warning sirens and their ability to provide a timely warning of impending storm danger. The commissioners had solicited a bid for the installation of the system, but for the past three years had resisted the project, suggesting the tight budget did not allow the expenditure. A federal grant application had arrived, and was in Commissioner Sadinski's desk. The grant would provide ninety percent of the funding for the project, but Sadinski's attempt to entice his brother-in-law to set up a subsidiary to his residential electrical contracting company so that he could be awarded the installation contract was still in the works. Until that preliminary agenda item was complete, the grant application was kept in his locked desk drawer.

Boog left Stella at the information desk and headed for the boiler room to fetch a ladder and a long snatch pole to change a light bulb in the courthouse entrance hall. He planned to complete that chore and then retire to his office until the end of the day. The boiler room was his paradise. He had the walls covered with pegboards, and there was a complete inventory of hand tools at his disposal. Each tool had its own place on the board, its outline drawn in white, the tool description inscribed within the outline so if a tool went missing from its designated spot, one could merely look at the outline and description and know what tool had been taken. He had constructed a workbench of rough lumber with a vice and grinding wheel attached. The room was lit with overhead hanging fluorescent lights, and his pride and joy sat in the corner—an overstuffed easy chair someone had thrown in the dumpster behind the courthouse. With the exception of the sheriff and the commissioners, he was the only person with a key to the boiler room. He could sit in his easy chair and relax to his heart's content with the only potential for interruption being the courthouse intercom system.

At three-fifteen, after returning from changing the light bulb, Boog sat in his easy chair, browsing through a Cabela's catalogue, daydreaming about using the DHS boat to go bass fishing. He felt an unusual pressure in his ears, reminiscent of his plane trip to Washington as the plane descended for landing. His ears popped once and then again. The fluorescent light fixtures made the slightest swaying motion, blinked, and then went out, and he heard a distant rumble, not unlike thunder, but lasting too long, too consistently. He glanced at the battery-operated clock hanging next to the door and decided to wander up to his office and find out why the power went off.

The pounding on the door was dramatic and pierced by Stella screaming his name. "Boog, Boog, open the door. Oh, my God. Oh, my God, Boog, please." Having found a battery-operated flashlight, he rushed and threw the bolt and opened the door. Stella fell through the opening into his arms. Blood was streaming down her face onto her blouse and she continued to scream. "Oh, my God. Oh, my God."

Boog pushed her back, trying to identify her injury. She had glass particles throughout her hair, and the blood streamed from small lacerations on her face. "What happened? Stella, calm down, and tell me what happened."

"Oh, my God; it's awful. I don't know what—I mean, oh, my God. I heard all this noise and went to look out, and the window smashed in my face. It was as if a bomb went off. Oh, my God." She seemed to calm for an instant and then shrieked, "My kids! Oh, God, my kids." She pushed him back and ran from the room and down the hall sobbing and continuing to scream, "Oh, my God, my kids."

Boog followed her, running behind. When they reached the stairs leading to the first-floor level, he heard screaming and crying. They ran up the stairs, entering the hall to the main lobby. As they got to the lobby, the floor became covered with broken glass and other debris. He followed Stella as she sprinted toward the back exit of the courthouse. When they got to the door, it became obvious the door was blocked from the outside. The plate glass was broken and a large metal object leaned against the door, darkening the exit. He saw what looked like inverted lettering. Then it hit him. It was the stenciled "H" of the DHS on top of his trailer that used to be parked in the courthouse parking lot but was now pushed up against the doorway.

Stella turned, pushed him out of the way again, and started running back into the building, apparently looking for another way out, her motherly instincts taking command over her initial hysteria. In the main lobby, there were traumatized employees walking around aimlessly, apparently unsure of what had happened. Sufficient light streamed in through the broken windows to reveal a chaotic picture of broken glass and strewn papers from the intense wind. Boog stopped at a broken window that gave a view of the parking lot. Cars were piled on top of one another. The boat and four-wheeler were not visible, but the Hummer was still on its wheels, another vehicle on its side leaning against it.

Boog yelled at Stella's back as she ran for the front entrance of the courthouse. "I'll go get the keys to the Hummer and meet you in the parking lot." He heard sirens start to blare through the open windows as he ran up the stairs to his office. At the third-floor level, he took a brief moment to look out the window at the end of the hall. The landscape looked like a war zone. The buildings left standing, mostly masonry, had all their windows blown out and trees leaning against them. The streets and parking lots visible from the window were littered with debris and overturned cars, toppled trees, and disoriented people.

He grabbed the keys and sprinted for the parking lot. Exiting the building, he passed people sitting in open areas, holding children, crying, and some asking for help to find family members. The courthouse parking lot was a jumbled mess of cars piled against each other. Some people were pushing debris off their cars while others were actually crashing out of the lot by pushing other cars out of the way with their own.

Stella came running across the lot, yelling for him to hurry. "My car is on its side. We have to take the Hummer." She sprinted over to the Hummer. The boat trailer was leaning against the passenger side of the Hummer. The boat lay at the other end of the parking lot wedged between two cars. They climbed in the Hummer through the driver side door, and Boog started the motor. He flipped on the emergency lights and siren and pulled away from the trailer, at first dragging it alongside with it eventually becoming dislodged as they made it to the street.

"My mother's house. They're at my mother's house," she screamed over the blaring siren.

Boog surveyed the street in both directions. Stella's mother's house was about five blocks from the courthouse, not far from the school, but the streets were completely blocked by fallen trees, debris, and numerous cars. He turned left and received a stern reproach from Stella. "It's closer the other way. Turn right. Turn right. Go down Main to Sycamore." She reached for the wheel to make him turn, but he grabbed her hand.

"This will be faster. There is too much stuff in the road that way. We'll never get through. We might be able to cut through some parking lots this way." After only a few hundred yards, they found the street blocked by a tree lying over two cars. He backed up and tried to push his way through the top of the tree, but hit a major limb. He stopped and surveyed the problem, threw the Hummer in reverse, and charged back down the street. He found an entry onto the sidewalk and started back toward the obstruction. This time, he found a space between two cars that had been pushed off the street and rammed one enough to spin it out of the way. They progressed another half-block before coming upon a power line that was arcing and spraying sparks into the street. There was no way to tell which wire was hot because an entire power pole had fallen across the street and several wires were lying limp in the tangle of tree limbs and debris. An alleyway between two buildings appeared to be clear, and Boog charged through the opening.

Once off the business district street they entered a more residential area, and the devastation made Stella begin to weep again as she held her hand to her mouth. Houses were toppled at worst; at best, their roofs had been blow away. Trees, those still standing, were completely stripped of any leaves, but in most cases, just the main trunk remained. People were starting to gather in groups, trying to grasp the immensity of the devastation, and preparing to look for those missing.

As they slowly progressed, going around or over downed trees, taking note of the destroyed houses, Stella began to whisper the Lord's Prayer. When she finished, she crossed herself, covered her face with her hands, and sobbed, whispering, "Please, God, save my children. Please, God, save my children."

From a block away, Stella's mother's house came into view. It was a one and a half-story Cape Cod-style before the storm. Now it was one-story, the roof pancaked down on the ground floor. There was no visible activity as they approached. Fallen trees prohibited them from getting into the yard, and before Boog could stop the Hummer, Stella jumped from the truck and ran toward the house, climbing over limbs and struggling through the debris, yelling, "Eric, Erin, Mom, where are you? Oh, God, say something. Where are you?"

Boog jumped from the truck and ran to catch up. There was a faint odor of sulfur in the air, indicating a natural gas leak in the vicinity, but otherwise, there was pervasive serenity that only those in the aftermath of intense destruction can describe.

Stella reached the porch first. The roof of the covered porch was leaning precariously, having been pushed forward when the roof collapsed. It appeared that the roof had been lifted off the house and dropped back down, collapsing the supporting rafters. The front door remained closed, and Stella ducked under the sagging porch roof and pounded on the door again, calling her children's names as she sobbed in desperation.

Boog moved to the side of the house, and after moving a large, fallen tree branch, cupped his hands, and peered into one of the few unbroken windows. The ceiling of the living room was collapsed with wooden joist hanging down, cracked, and splintered. Debris obscured his view into any other areas of the house, and as he pulled away to search for another entry point, he heard a faint call. "Mommy, Mommy." It was followed by the cry of the youngest child.

He yelled to Stella. "I hear them, but I can't tell where they are. Do you hear them?"

Stella came around the corner of the house, plowing through tree limbs like a sow bear charging to protect her cubs. "Where are they? Are they in that room?" She reached the window and shoved him aside, cupping her hands at the window. She heard the crying and the pleading yell for Mommy. "Oh, God," she said to herself and then yelled, "Mommy's here; I'm coming to get you. Where's Grammy? Is she with you?"

They waited for a reply, but only heard the sobbing cry of the scared child.

She pushed back from the window and looked at him. "I've got to get in there. They must be in the basement. The stairs to the basement are in the kitchen in the back of the house." She bolted from the window, plowing through more debris toward the back of the house, Boog trailing at her heels. The broken points of the limbs tore at her dress as she half-climbed, half-burrowed through the mess. The back porch was mostly intact, and they scampered up the steps. Stella pulled at the screen door, and although it buckled and bent under the pressure, it opened. Next, she grasped the door handle and found the wooden door unlocked, but it would not budge. Apparently, the house had shifted under the pressure of the collapse and jammed the door. She pushed with her shoulder, but there was no give. Boog stepped forward and tried the same thing without success. They both stepped back and surveyed their options.

"Let's break that window and go in that way," Stella said, not waiting for a substantive reaction from him. She ran down the steps, grabbed a chuck of tree limb lying on the ground, and pitched it through the kitchen window, shattering the glass. She began searching for something to stand on to give her enough lift to get her through the window. Boog realized he had to slow her down and reason with her.

"Stella, let me go in, look around, try to find them and determine what needs to be done to get them out. You take the truck and try to find help. We may need an ambulance or the fire department to get them out." She wasn't responding to his words; she was dragging a lawn chair through the debris toward the window. He saw it was useless to reason with her and went to help her drag the chair. "Okay, if you aren't going to go, then let me go in first and try to find them. Someone will have to stay out here and help when I lift them out." They had the chair at the window, and she looked at him, the blood clotted on her face, staining her hair, which was matted against her scalp.

"Jasper Simpson, those are my children, and they are calling for me. They need me. I will give you five minutes then I am coming in." He had never seen a more intense or motivated look on her face.

"Help me through the window. Give me a push once I get up on the chair, and get my shoulders through the window." He stepped up on the chair, picked some of the remaining glass away from the bottom of the window and around the side, and hoisted himself up. Stella gave him a push from behind, and he fell through the window, landing on the floor. He rolled over and sat looking at the dark room, letting his eyes adjust, trying to determine where the doors and hallways led.

Stella poked her head in the window as far as she could reach, standing on the chair. "The basement door is over there."

She pointed at the opposite corner of the kitchen where the refrigerator stood, holding the collapsed ceiling up. Two by fours torn from the rafters were crossed in front of the refrigerator; chunks of plaster and insulation hung like tattered flesh. The crying had stopped, but they could hear one of the children sobbing.

Stella cried, “Erin, is that you? Where’s Grammy?”

“Mommy, Mommy, we’re in the basement. The door is broken, and there’s stuff on the stairs. Hurry, it’s dark down here.” Both children started crying again.

“Where’s Grammy?” Stella asked again.

“She’s lying down. She doesn’t feel good.”

Boog crawled toward the basement door. He pushed one broken two by four out of the way, allowing plaster and debris to funnel through a large hole in the ceiling down on top of him. Other broken beams and ceiling joists were lodged, blocking the doorway. He stood and tried to move them without success. His efforts did release pressure on the broken timber, offering an ominous moan as the collapsed roof shifted above him. He squeezed through two crossed and broken pieces of lumber and reached the door. The ceiling rested on top of the refrigerator and sagged, making it impossible to open the basement door.

Stella yelled from the window, “Can you open the door? Is it stuck?”

“The door is jammed. The ceiling is hanging down too far. It won’t open.”

There was a crack, and the floor and walls shook as a portion of the roof fell further into the front of the house. The air from the implosion rushed out of the broken windows, pressing dust into Stella’s eyes. The air in the kitchen was heavy with a cloud of brown dust as she rubbed her eyes and tried to see Boog across the room.

Desperation in her voice, she yelled, “You all right? Boog, answer me. You all right?”

"Yeah, I just can't see anything. It's so dusty. I'm going to try to break through the door." He crawled closer to the door and positioned himself, sitting, leaning against his arms, gaining as much leverage as possible in his legs, and kicked at the bottom panel of the door. At first, it did not give at all. It was a solid wood door and dated back to the original construction of the house, but after repeated kicks, the bottom panel of the door started to buckle and break away. As he kicked and broke away the bottom of the door, it became apparent that the door, door jam, and the refrigerator were the only support for the sagging ceiling and upper collapsed roof. More debris crashed down from above, and the menacing creaks of stressed wood made him stop, wait, and think about what to do next.

"Can you see them? What are you doing? I'm coming in. Are you all right?"

He heard Stella grunting, trying to pull herself up into the window.

"Don't come in. It's too dangerous. This place could collapse at anytime. Your movement could make it come down. Just stay there. I'm going through the door into the basement. I'll bring them out soon. Just stay there." He cautiously drew closer to the door, keeping a close eye on the hanging tangle of lumber and plaster above him. The hole he had kicked out was just large enough for him to squeeze through feet first. He pushed himself through, rolling over on his stomach, and felt the decline of the staircase. Glass jars and other debris crashed down the stairs as he bumped down the first few steps before grabbing the handrail and stopping himself. The basement was dark with only a few streams of light entering through a small window well on a far facing wall.

"Mommy, is that you?" The question was a hushed whisper.

"No, it's Boog. Remember me? I'm here to take you to your mother. She is outside waiting. Are you guys all right? Anybody hurt?" As his eyes further adjusted to the darkness, he saw two small forms huddled at the bottom of the stairs. An occasional sob interrupted the silence. "Okay, I'm coming down now. Stay back, because there is stuff on the stairs that might fall down. Where's Grammy?"

Erin, the oldest daughter, said, "She's over in the corner, sleeping. Something flew through the window when she looked out, and she went to sleep."

"Okay, let's see if we can get up these stairs and go through the hole in the door. I want you to come to me, okay? Eric, you come first, then Erin, okay? When we get to the top of the stairs, I will crawl through the hole, and then you follow me. Mommy is right outside, and she will help you out the window."

From the window, he heard Stella start to scream. "Jasper Simpson, you answer me. What are you doing? Did you find them? I'm coming in."

He cupped his hand at his mouth and yelled, directing his voice toward the hole in the door. "We're all right. We're coming out. Stay at the window so you can lift them out."

The next question was not as easy to answer.

"Where's my mom? Is she all right?"

He hesitated, not knowing the answer. "Let's get the kids out first." He turned and found them both at his heels on the stairs. "Okay, I'm going to go through this hole in the door. You come through after me, and I will lift you out of the window." He turned and started pulling himself through the hole. There was a sudden shuddering, and another rumble sent a cloud of dust through the kitchen. Chunks of plaster fell on his back as he pulled himself through the hole, and then it seemed like the entire ceiling caved in with a wicked cracking of lumber and the deep moaning sound of a manmade structure pressed beyond its breaking point. He was halfway through the hole, covered with debris from the falling ceiling, and more cracked and splintered lumber had littered the path to the window. He clawed at the floor and shook off the chunks of plaster that had landed on his back. There was no room to stand now, and only a small space where he thought they could crawl under the rubble. A kitchen table that had been standing when he passed through the kitchen before was now collapsed and covered with debris.

Once through the hole, he turned and pulled the first child through and then the next. They were all on their hands and knees, and he surveyed the room. The refrigerator still held up part of the ceiling near them but the balance of the room was completely filled with the remains of the upper half-story of the house. It appeared that they might be able to crawl around the outside of the room near the partition wall and get to the window.

He turned and looked at the two children and smiled. Amazingly, they smiled back. Their rescue had become a game, and they had apparently lost their fear.

"Okay, everyone ready?" They responded with another smile. "Let's slither like snakes." He got down on his stomach and began pulling himself through the debris, gently moving as much of the rubble as possible. It was easier than he had anticipated, and after a few feet, he saw Stella's head sticking through the window. "Here we come, safe and sound."

Boog lifted Eric up to his mother, and she pulled him through the window, tears streaming down her face, and smothered him with kisses. Next came Erin, to the same ecstatic reception.

"I'm going back down stairs to get your mother." He turned and started crawling back under the rubble.

Stella stuck her head back in the window and asked, "Where is she? Is she all right?" But all she saw was the bottom of his boots as he crawled away. He did not answer.

She sat in the grass, holding her children as close as she could, not talking, but silently thanking God for answering her prayer and thinking about how she would cherish each future moment with Boog and her children when he and her mother were finally out of the house. Coming this close to losing her family brought her a calming, surreal realization of the loving relationship she had established with Jasper Simpson.

A spring breeze arose in the aftermath of the storm, and the young leaves on the fallen tree limbs shimmered and danced around the three sitting on the ground holding each other. Suddenly, the old house groaned, and with a staggering *farrump,* the entire remaining structure collapsed into the basement. A cloud of dust billowed into the air, swirled in the light breeze, and then there was silence.

Epilogue

Associated Press, April 28; Hinkley County, IL: *Local DHS Director Dies Saving Children*

The Hinkley County, Illinois Department of Homeland Security director, Jasper Simpson, was killed while rescuing two children from a collapsed dwelling following a devastating tornado. Simpson was one of thirteen fatalities from the storm that spawned eight tornados across the Midwest on Thursday. According to Hinkley County sheriff, Reginald Minor, Simpson had crawled into a collapsed dwelling after hearing the cries of a child and rescued the children of Stella O'Reilly before going back into the house for another victim. During the failed second rescue attempt, the house collapsed, killing Simpson. It was later determined that the second victim, Margaret Meadows, the mother of Stella O'Reilly, was already deceased from an injury sustained during the storm. The storm damage in Hinkley County alone has been estimated to exceed fifteen million dollars. Officials in Hinkley County said they were still waiting to hear from the Federal Emergency Management Agency, managed by the Department of Homeland Security, with regard to federal assistance with the cleanup.

Simpson left a legacy of gallant acts during his short term as local director of the Hinkley County Department of Homeland Security. He had recently been recognized by his peers at the Department of Homeland Security National Directors' meeting for heroic actions at the local high school after a hazardous material spill. Acting Secretary of Homeland Security Rueben Feinstein said, "Jasper Simpson was an example of the dedicated citizens working for the department all across our country, performing selfless acts of heroism that are many times unrecognized unless there is a tragic outcome. We honor Mister Simpson; he is a true American hero." Hinkley County Commissioner Chet Sadinski paid tribute to Simpson by saying,

"Jasper Simpson was like a son to me. He was known as a kind and generous member of our courthouse family and will be sorely missed."

Although funeral arrangements are incomplete for Simpson, the ceremony is expected to draw attendance from high-ranking federal officials.

***Hinkley Messenger*; April 29**
Director Dies Saving Children

Well-known county director of homeland security, Jasper Simpson, died during a heroic attempt to rescue trapped victims of Thursday's storm. Simpson rescued the children of Stella O'Reilly from her mother's home and had re-entered the dwelling to retrieve the body of Margaret Meadows, who it was later determined had died as a result of injuries received during the storm. The structure collapsed during the ill-fated second rescue attempt. Simpson and Meadows' bodies were found in the basement of the collapsed dwelling and were extracted from the rubble late Thursday night after a large backhoe was brought to the scene. The bodies were taken to the temporary morgue set up in the walk-in cooler at the Super Value on South Main Street.

Simpson had been nationally recognized for his heroic efforts after a hazardous waste spill at Hinkley High School last fall. He was awarded a presidential citation, and local officials applauded his actions and said he saved the school and county thousands of dollars in cleanup costs.

Jasper Simpson was a life-long resident of Hinkley County and had worked for the county for over fifteen years before being promoted to the position of director of Hinkley County Homeland Security. Board of Commissioners' president Chet Sadinski said of Simpson, "It is difficult to put into words the loss we, the commissioners, our staff, and everyone who knew Boog—that was his nickname—feel at this time. He was one of our most dedicated and well liked employees."

Jasper Simpson graduated from Hinkley High School, and until his promotion to director of Homeland Security for Hinkley County, had been the Hinkley County courthouse custodian.

Funeral services for Jasper Simpson are incomplete at this time.

Hinkley Messenger, Obituary, Jasper Simpson
JASPER (BOOGER) SIMPSON

Jasper Simpson, age 42, died the afternoon of April 27 from injuries sustained during a search and rescue effort. Jasper Simpson was born in Hinkley County on October 21, 1965 to Grazelda Mayberry and Frank Simpson. Grazelda Mayberry preceded him in death in 1973. Grandparents Raymond and Effy Mayberry, who preceded him in death, raised Jasper. There is no record of siblings or other relatives.

Simpson was employed as the director of Homeland Security for Hinkley County. He was a graduate of Hinkley High School and is scheduled to be inducted into the Hinkley High School Hall of Fame at the Hinkley High School graduation ceremony in May of this year. The award will be given posthumously.

Arrangements are by Roberts Funeral Home/Crematorium and Florist.

There will be no visitation. A service will be held at the Body of Christ on the Cross Baptist Church, Wednesday at 1:00 PM. The body will be cremated.

Stella sat in the front row in the sanctuary of the Body of Christ on the Cross Baptist Church. She wore a tight, black knit sweater with long sleeves and carried a matching black purse. She didn't own a black skirt, so charcoal gray had to do. She held the purse in one hand and grasped Eric's small hand with the other. Next to Eric sat Erin, then Eddy, and finally Bud, squirming uncomfortably, trying to maneuver inside a suit coat that was at least two sizes too small and ten years old. Stella leaned forward, looking down the pew at Bud, and with a steely gaze and gritted teeth whispered, "Take that damned hat off."

The organ moaned a funeral dirge in anticipation of a long day of grieving for Stella and most of her family. Following the service for Boog, the grieving would continue for her mother with visitation scheduled at Roberts Funeral Home. Fellow courthouse employees filed into the sanctuary, still in shock and temporarily displaced from work while the courthouse remained closed for repairs and the community slowly recovered from the devastating storm.

Pastor Butterbetter entered the sanctuary as the clock ticked one o'clock, and he approached the altar, but rather than ascend the few steps, he walked around and stood next to the three legged pedestal topped by the urn containing Boog's remains. He bowed his head in a prayerful repose before beginning the service.

"Friends, we are gathered here to celebrate the glorious ascension of our brother Jasper Booger Simpson to the heavenly gates of eternal life. God sent his only son, Jesus Christ, to die for our sins, and today, brother Boog joins him, to live eternally at the right hand of God the Father. Can I hear an amen? Can I hear a 'blessed be the righteous'? Thank you, friends. You might today ask, why has God brought this devastation to our community? Why has God taken this fine young man in the prime of his life, in the midst of a courageous act? Friends, you will find the answer in prayer. When you feel forsaken, when you feel you are on the precipice of eternal damnation for your sins, when there does not seem to be light at the end of the tunnel, God will answer you, he will guide you; he will give you salvation and lead you to be born again. Just pray, my friends, just pray. In the midst of the devastation this community has endured, God saved this building as an example of the power of prayer. Can I hear an amen? Can I hear a blessed be the righteous?" Pastor Butterbetter raised his hands, dispensed with a seemingly never-ending prayer, and upon conclusion, said, "Is there anyone present who would like to speak, to express a joy about our brother Boog?"

As Pastor Butterbetter's final words bounced off the final wall, the silence in the sanctuary became deep, almost cavernous. Slowly, Stella leaned forward and rose from her seat, the knots in her stomach so tense she could not stand straight, and as she turned to face the congregation, she had to steady herself, holding on to the back of the pew. Eric stood, as if on cue, and wrapped his arms around his mother's waist, half-holding and half-hugging.

"Over the past year," Stella hesitated as her own words bounced back at her in the large hall, "I've gotten to know Boog, become close—." Stella began to sob. "I mean, many of you saw him as our janitor, but he was so, so much more. He was the kindest, gentlest, most honest—" She dabbed her eyes with a tissue. "Smartest—"

Stella heard a chuckle from somewhere in the back, and she sternly redressed the crowd. "Yes, I said smartest. He may not have gone to college like a lot of you, but he knew things about life, things that you can't learn in books. He didn't want all the attention, the awards—" Her tears began flowing. "He just wanted to do what's right. He cared about his job, he cared about this community, and he just, just—" She sank down in the pew with her head in her arms, crying. "He just cared so much; he cared so much, so much…" Her voice faded, and she sobbed into her own arms.

Pastor Butterbetter came over to the pew and placed a hand on Stella's shoulder. "Let us pray."

The service concluded with six verses of "Amazing Grace" and a reminder from Pastor Butterbetter that there was a collection plate at the end of each aisle for those who wanted to participate in the Body of Christ on the Cross Baptist Church special capital campaign to replace the aging parsonage that was miraculously spared from damage by the recent storm, much to Pastor Butterbetter's chagrin.

As the sanctuary slowly cleared, Stella asked Bud to take the children to Roberts Funeral Home so she could have some time alone at the altar. Bud squirmed, hesitated, suggested he had some errands to run, then melted under Stella's steel gaze and relented. When the sanctuary had cleared and again become quiet, she approached the altar and knelt, crossing herself, and silently prayed.

Finished with her meditation, she stared at the urn on the pedestal in front of her, thinking about the future she and Boog could have shared and the unjust finality of the last few days. Just when she felt she could cry no more, tears welled in her eyes and lazily traversed her cheeks. Rising and composing herself again, she contemplated taking the urn with her, but decided against it, realizing there was no one else that cared or would come for the remains before she had time to return. She wiped her eyes, took one last look at the stoic urn, symbolizing so much, but meaning so little, turned, and started down the aisle toward the exit.

Roger Witherspoon stood at the rear of the sanctuary, leaning against the last pew. "Stella, can I talk to you for a minute?"

Witherspoon, an attorney with the firm Witherspoon and Witherspoon, was a well-known face around the courthouse in Hinkley County, spending the majority of his career as a public defender and occupying a small office next to Ralphy's on Main Street. When not defending the underprivileged, he generally held court on the end stool at Ralphy's bar.

Stella stopped when she saw Witherspoon, hesitated, and responded, "Not now, Roger; I don't have time." Since her divorce, Witherspoon had twice approached her for a date, for which she had no interest, and she assumed he was seizing the opportunity again.

"This will only take a minute, and I am awfully sorry about this. I know you and Boog were close."

Stella walked closer, smelling the alcohol that he had probably consumed over lunch, and decided that if he hit on her again, she was going to respond with a swift kick to the crotch, church or no church. After all, she wasn't Baptist, she was

Catholic, and forgiveness was only a half-mile away. She gave him a stern look. “I have to go, Roger; my family is waiting, and I have another funeral to go to.”

“I understand, but there is something you should know.”

She tried to pass, but Roger gently put his hand on her shoulder. “Just listen for a minute, please.”

Stella stopped, released an exhaustive sigh and gave in, too tired to argue.

“Boog came to see me a few weeks ago, and well, he was planning for the future. Stell, my guess is that he was thinking about marriage.” He paused to let the last statement be absorbed. Stella opened her eyes wide and stared at Witherspoon in astonishment. “Anyway, he wanted you to have something; I mean, if anything ever happened to him.”

Stella continued her blank stare, still apprehensive about Witherspoon’s motive, not focusing, trying to hold back tears, and gathered the strength to whisper her reply with a sharp edge. “What is it he wanted me to have, Roger?”

“Well, there is his county employee life insurance. You are the beneficiary, and it’s double indemnity for accidental death. That’s twenty thousand dollars. He mentioned something about your kids’ education, not that he was expecting to collect this soon, of course.”

She turned, grasped the end of the pew for balance, and with a thump, sat down. “Twenty thousand dollars. Oh, Boog, Boog.” She rested her face in her hands as the tears flowed.

“Stell, there’s more. He had me make a will naming you as the beneficiary, inheriting all of his possessions. It all goes to you.” Stella continued to sob and he sat down next to her and placed his hand on her shoulder. “You know how Boog was, Stell. Hell, he never spent a dime on anything—lived over Hanover’s hardware store for years. He never paid any rent as long as he kept the place swept up, didn’t own a car. Anyway, the way I understand it, years ago, Tug Longwater, he kind of watched over Boog after his parents were gone, he set up an account for him with Jerry Smith, the investment guy over at the State Bank, and most of his check went right into that account. You ever hear of Microsoft, Stell? Anyway, Boog just gave me the account number when we talked and I never paid any attention until this happened. I checked yesterday and that account is worth over eight hundred and twenty five thousand dollars."

Stella bent over and threw up on her Hushpuppies.

The end.

Printed in the United States
133099LV00002B/85-96/P

9 781605 940830